"Say you'll marry me now. Or I'll have to walk out of your life forever."

"That sounds like an ultimatum."

"It is. I'm not going through this again," Trader replied. "You're in a unique position to change my life."

The money would change his life, Claire thought sadly. "Trader—" she began, but his finger stopped her lips.

"If you doubt me, if you reject me now, I'm not hanging around for an encore.... Yes, or no?"

Childhood in Portsmouth meant grubby knees, flying pigtails and happiness for *SARA WOOD*. Poverty drove her from typist and seaside landlady to teacher till writing finally gave her the freedom her Romany blood craved. Sara is happily married and has two handsome adult sons, Richard and Simon. She lives in the Cornish countryside. Sara's glamorous writing life alternates with her passion for gardening, which allows her to be carefree and grubby again.

Books by Sara Wood

HARLEQUIN PRESENTS
1765—SHADES OF SIN
1790—TANGLED DESTINIES
1796—UNCHAINED DESTINIES
1802—THREADS OF DESTINY

SARA WOOD

Second-Best Bride

Harlequin Books

TORONTO • NEW YORK • LONDON
AMSTERDAM • PARIS • SYDNEY • HAMBURG
STOCKHOLM • ATHENS • TOKYO • MILAN
MADRID • WARSAW • BUDAPEST • AUCKLAND

ISBN 0-373-11817-1

SECOND-BEST BRIDE

First North American Publication 1996.

Copyright © 1995 by Sara Wood.

CHAPTER ONE

IT SHOULD have been the happiest day of her life, not the worst. Weren't weddings supposed to make people cry with joy? Claire felt closer to howling, and joy didn't come into it. Misery, yes. Disillusionment. Self-pity and embarrassment. Not much cause to laugh there.

She huddled deeper into the corner of the limousine, staring at the billows of ivory taffeta where her voluminous skirt had been spread carefully over the cream leather seat. And she wondered how on earth she could bring herself to speak. The words were quite simple. No long syllables to tangle a tongue. 'I can't marry Trader'. So why did they ball up together and stick in her throat?

A sour-tasting sickness heaved and rolled in her stomach. She closed her soft-green eyes tightly and counted slowly to ten till the nausea went away. After her hen party, she should have gone home. Disastrously for her peace of mind, she'd let Phoenix persuade her to stay on for a couple of brandies and an intimate chat.

Big mistake. Better to have remained ignorant. Her tongue slicked nervously over her dry lips, removing the final traces of peach lipstick. All night she'd dwelt on the things Phoenix had said till she'd been half tearing her hair out with despair.

She stole a look in her father's direction. He was a picture of contentment: a handsome man, his un-

familiar face glowing with anticipation. Daunted by
his delight, Claire couldn't quite pluck up the courage
to tell him the bad news.

Her heart thudded away while the smooth, osten-
tatious limousine purred along with its mockery of
fluttering satin ribbons on the endless bonnet. They
were alarmingly near to the grey stone church. And
Trader. And the hundreds of guests. A hot wave swept
over her.

'We're late,' commented her father crossly. 'Your
fault. Good crowd, mind.' His hand crossed her vision
in a flash of gold and ruby rings, waving royally. 'It's
their entertainment, I suppose,' he grunted, with all
the contempt of a Channel Islander for the unsophisticated people of remote Ballymare. 'I suppose weddings and funerals add drama to their drab, small
lives.'

They'd get drama, thought Claire. This would be
a wedding and a funeral rolled up in one! And oh,
the shame of it! She shuddered. Faint from skittering
nerves, she placed her hand on her father's arm,
flinching at the ragged, good-natured cheer that arose
outside when the car slowly drew up to the kerb.

Deep breath. Calm voice. Firm, decisive. 'Don't get
out! I can't go through with the wedding!' she cried
shakily, forcing the words through her pale, dry lips
in a sudden, gabbling rush.

'*Whaaat*? Sweetie——!' Her father reached to grab
her trembling hand and she withdrew it, backing away
warily.

'No!' she said huskily. 'I won't budge! I won't
change my mind!'

'The woman's mad!' Her father took one close look
at her set face and his mouth went grim. 'Driver! Go

round the block again! Claire, what are you trying to do, give me a coronary? I'll make you marry Trader if I have to carry you——'

'I think the guests might notice if the bride arrives struggling and screaming over your shoulder,' she retorted defiantly, finding his idea ridiculous. She was close to laughing hysterically—or was she nearer to tears? Whatever. Far too many emotions were thrashing around in her head. 'I'm sorry,' she went on sympathetically. 'I really am. But my mind's made up.'

'Well, unmake it. Are you nuts?' asked her father aggressively.

'No,' she said forlornly. 'Sane at last.'

'But it's been "Trader, Trader, Trader" ever since I arrived in Ireland five days ago! You're nervous, that's all. Snap out of it, sweetie!' Seeing her set mouth, her father changed tack, holding back his temper and turning on the charm that had coaxed a lifetime of women into his arms, hissing the words through perfectly capped teeth. 'Of course you'll go through with it! Honeymoon in the Seychelles, palm trees, blue skies, hot sun... The expense! The marquee alone cost——'

'I know. A fortune. You told me.' She gave a faint, sad smile. His materialistic nature always surfaced. 'I'm terribly sorry to do this to you!' Her huge eyes pleaded with him in vain for comfort. 'Dad——'

He scowled. '*Jack*. I told you! I don't like being reminded that I'm old enough to be the father of a twenty-two-year-old woman. Now shape up,' he snapped. 'Fast.'

'That's the trouble. I've shaped,' she muttered.

And felt very alone. A cuddle and some understanding would be nice. But Jack only played the one role: that of a macho charmer. Sadly she took in the dyed black waves and incongruously unlined face. Plastic surgery had meant that her father bore little resemblance to the photograph by her mother's bedside. It was the face of a stranger.

And Trader was a stranger too, she realised with an awful jolt, twisting her long, slender fingers in alarm. Sunlight shafted in through the window, lighting her pale face and lowered golden lashes, glancing off the facets of the diamonds and emeralds of her engagement ring. It had been hers for barely a week; dreams discovered, dreams realised ... Dreams lost? Her breath caught in her throat and she had to fight not to break down.

'Jack. Please understand,' she said quietly. 'I can't marry Trader. I know it's the eleventh hour. I know it's embarrassing and annoying and it'll cause a lot of trouble if I back out—but I'd rather cope with the flak than marry and have regrets for the rest of my life, or be driven to divorce. I never once stopped to think things through,' she explained. 'It's been such a whirl. He never let up once, never left me alone,' she added helplessly. 'Trader bulldozed me.'

And she'd allowed it! Secretly, she was appalled. Always thoughtful, always reticent to the point of silence, she'd never let her feelings run away with her so drastically. How *could* she be marrying someone she'd only known for three weeks?

'Trader's like that. Single-minded. Beats you over the head till he gets what he wants,' grunted Jack.

'How do you know?' Claire frowned. 'You only met him a few days ago.'

'We talked business a few times,' said her father curtly.

'Business?' she queried. 'I thought you disliked one another. Did you chat together while I was working at the hotel?'

'We do loathe the sight of each other,' Jack acknowledged. 'But that's got nothing to do with it. It's too late to change your mind. You've *got* to be nice to him——'

'I've *what*?' she said sharply, unsure she'd heard correctly.

Grim and suddenly old behind the unnaturally youthful face, Jack said testily, 'Be a good girl and treat him well! Do whatever he wants! Don't cross him, Claire. There'll be trouble.'

'*Trouble*? Isn't that being a bit melodramatic?' she asked in astonishment.

'I wish!' said her father gloomily. 'Take it from one who knows. Handle him with kid gloves. The man's dynamite on legs. He'll detonate just for spite. Marry him. For my sake. For your own.'

Fear drained even the effects of blusher on her pale, fine-boned face. Behind the hazy silk of her veil, her eyes looked like two huge mossy smudges as she stared back at her father. 'I *knew* Trader was holding something back! I knew he wasn't telling me everything, that he had a secret!' she said tremulously. 'Tell me what's going on! I'm sitting in this car till you do!'

'Oh God!' he groaned. He was silent for a while and she felt like screaming when he hesitated for interminable seconds. 'OK,' he said heavily. 'I'm in trouble. We've both got to crawl in whichever direction he orders. He's calling the tune and I'm dancing. You're part of the package. Let him have you!'

'A *package*!' Taut in every muscle, Claire leaned forward and let her father's words roll around her head till they sank in fully. Her lips tightened into a searingly thin line.

'Yeah. Bastard's got a hold on me as tight as a ferret.'

'You do mean *Trader*?' she asked faintly. Her stomach gave a lurch again and her small hand flew to the tightly fitting bodice as if it could hold back the swelling misery inside.

'Trader,' confirmed her father bitterly. 'Trader-blasted-Benedict! Terminator bloody III!'

'She's late.'

Trader scowled at his best man's obvious remark. 'Bride's privilege,' he said curtly.

'Ye-e-es. Sure this is right for you?' asked Charles with a wise caution. Trader had been edgy all morning. 'You could walk out now——'

'And miss out on the chance of a lifetime?' growled Trader. His head turned with an angry jerk and his eyes raked the aisle grimly. If she didn't turn up, he'd crucify that father of hers and spread his entrails across their agreement.

An elegant, gloved hand fluttered, attracting his attention. Phoenix. He smiled faintly at her beautiful face, admiring the perfect make-up, noting with approval her air of sophistication and grooming. Phoenix blew him a kiss and he grinned, his black eyes dancing with the love he felt for her. Fee's features softened as they always did.

He raised a sardonic eyebrow and his broad shoulders, as if to say, 'Will she, won't she?' and Fee gave him a secretive smile. Because they sure shared one hell of a secret. And as he turned back, he hoped to God no one found out before he was well and truly married to Claire.

The bottomless pit of anger inside him surged up and quickened his breathing, the bitterness of twenty or more years ripping through him till he saw nothing but a red haze before his eyes.

It had gone on long enough. It had begun to cripple his life, threatening to taint the woman he loved. Trader forced himself to focus clearly on the altar rail and make a decision. Ten more minutes. After that he'd leave. And blow the whistle on Jack Jardine.

The cruel smile hardened his granite profile and his long-time friend, Charles Fairchild, shifted uncomfortably. Trader had always been complex, with a dark side he'd never dared to investigate. 'Bear up. She's worth the wait,' he said brightly.

Trader shot a quick look at the aisle and met Fee's affectionate eyes again. He relaxed and turned back to Charles. 'Yes,' he said softly. 'She is.'

'Driver! Go round again,' said Jack tensely as Claire slumped back into the seat and the crushed taffeta sighed all around her. 'Claire, you've got to help me!' he muttered. 'My whole business is on the line. Hundreds of my employees all over the world could be out of a job—and it would be your fault! I'm facing ruin!'

'From Trader? How? He's only known you a few days!' she exclaimed, bewildered by what was happening.

'We've just met. But he's been after me for years. Me and everything I have. Coveting it all! He doesn't care how he gets it.'

Claire gasped. 'But...what would he get from marrying me?'

'Half of everything I own,' Jack muttered, sounding utterly defeated.

'He gets *money* if I go through with this?' she asked with horror.

'Money. Property. Control. Half my wealth and possessions go to him as your dowry, I keep the rest.' Her father's mouth twisted bitterly. 'And in return he'll keep his mouth shut about my tax evasion and a couple of questionable deals. I owe several million dollars. That's a maximum three-hundred-year gaol sentence in America.'

'Three hundred...! Oh, Dad!' she moaned faintly. Now she understood! And Phoenix had been trying to warn her last night. Claire felt weak from shock. It was unbelievable that Trader could have betrayed her and lied so convincingly. A package! The idea rocked her to the core.

Her nagging doubts about the wisdom of their hasty marriage had turned into something really serious. Granted, she'd wanted to delay the marriage to straighten a few things out, but she hadn't bargained on being faced with an insurmountable obstacle like...like being betrothed to a man she couldn't respect. One who might not even love her.

'He—he said he loved me!' she ventured, a desperately hopeful note in her voice.

'Oh, sure he does!' affirmed her father, rather too painfully eager to convince her.

And she remarked with unusual cynicism, 'I suppose it can't be hard to love a blindly adoring woman with a tempting dowry.'

Her father shrugged. 'You get a lot out of this too. You share his half of the so-called dowry, after all. And I'm leaving you the other half when I die. You're an heiress, you know.'

Claire noted with sadness that he wasn't intending to leave anything to her mother. 'I hope you're not trying to buy my co-operation in this disgusting arrangement,' she said unhappily.

'You'd like to be rich,' he said sullenly. 'Everyone would.'

'I want enough money so that Mother doesn't have to work, that's all.' She thought for a moment. 'Does Trader know that, in addition to the dowry, I will eventually inherit your portion as well?' she asked slowly.

Her father nodded. 'He gets the lot eventually, one way or another. The whole Trebisonne empire. So what? He loves you, you love him. That's not so bad, is it?'

Claire groaned. 'Yes, it is! How can I marry a scheming rat?'

'Plenty of women do,' grunted her father. 'Why should you be so special?'

Because she wanted to fall in love and marry and be happy forever after. Because she wanted a husband who would walk over hot coals for her, cherish her in sickness and in health, forsaking all others till death them did part.

Not someone who'd put the screws on her father because he'd been fiddling his tax on a grand scale! Her father must be really desperate to give up half his wealth. He needed a lot of money for his extravagant lifestyle in Florida. The rejuvenating surgery alone must have cost thousands. And he'd let slip in a boast one day that he'd lost a million in Vegas. Expensive tastes.

'Trader didn't arrive in Ballymare by chance, did he?' she said harshly. 'It was no coincidence!'

'Coincidence? Are you joking?' scoffed her father incredulously.

Claire gave a little moan. She'd been set up. That meeting on the beach had been carefully planned. Trader was poor and he'd long coveted her father's money—so badly that he'd sink to blackmail to marry it. She'd known from the first that he'd needed to count the pennies. He wore nothing but comfortable old clothes and their time had been spent walking, talking, eating simple picnic food.

She gave a bitter smile. Because according to her aunts, her father had acquired the vast Le Trebisonne fitness centres by a cold-blooded and calculating second marriage to the widow of Philippe Le Trebisonne. And now the empire was being wrested from him by a man of equal cunning—ironically, also by marriage.

Trader and her father were unnervingly alike. And that horrified her. Two irresistible charmers. Both liars.

She winced. So much for being swept off her feet. Next time she'd apply Superglue.

'Marry him!' pleaded her father.

'You're asking me to sacrifice my future for you?' she asked with quiet dignity. 'You've only seen me twice in my life before this week. It's been fourteen years since you last came to Ballymare for a brief visit—and yet you're expecting my unquestioning loyalty!'

Her father's hand closed around her shoulder like a vice. 'If you *don't* marry him, Trader will bring the Revenue men down on me and the police and I'll lose everything. I want to be reconciled with your mother. She loves me——'

'Yes,' she said bitterly. 'Even though you walked out when she was pregnant with me, twenty-three years ago!' Her mother had loved her father through thick and thin, through infidelity, deceit, callousness. Inexplicable. But she knew that a reunion would make her mother overjoyed. Unfortunately, her father held the key to her mother's happiness.

More blackmail. And she was being drawn into it whether she liked it or not.

'We're here. Again,' grunted her father, leaping out. 'Get ready. Remember how ill your mother is.'

Pain sliced through her like a knife through butter. The door opened and the chauffeur's gloved hand stretched towards her. She stared at it blankly. But her father came around the car, pushed the concerned driver aside and grabbed Claire's slender wrist with a flash of chunky gold rings, hauling her out with an impatient, 'Too many people need this marriage. Get a hold on yourself and do your duty!'

Stunned by his lack of compassion, by his cruelty, she stumbled numbly a few yards down the church path through the crowds of friends and well-wishers. Words like 'fragile' and 'beautiful' and 'ethereal' came to her ears. For ethereal read shocked, she thought weakly.

Someone turned her around to pose for photographs. Hating to create a scene in public, she let herself be manhandled into position, silently enduring the embarrassment of the friendly compliments from everyone. Everyone loved a bride, she thought soberly. But...did the groom?

Trader was corrupt and grasping and he would change into a monster—as her father had—the minute she became his wife. Her mother had been fooled by Jack Jardine's easy charm. Why shouldn't she have inherited that blindness?

'Smile!' urged the photographer.

She did her best but her lips kept quivering. This was a farce! But it gave her time to think. 'A few more,' she suggested huskily.

Her hand fretted with a hairpin in her marmalade hair. Trader had likened it to a sheet of flamed water at sunset and said he loved it straight and hanging loose. But that morning Phoenix had organised it into alien curls heaped on her head and fixed with an arc of brutal grips. Claire felt like a prisoner, starting a gaol sentence. If only she'd waited and got to know Trader properly! But he could coax a polar bear to part with its fur...

'OK, that'll do.' Jack took her arm and squeezed it. 'This is it, sweetie,' he said shakily. 'Remember, I'd be no good to your mother in prison!'

Her face paled and she swallowed hard. Jack was her father, whatever his faults, and she couldn't blithely ignore his distress. All her life she'd longed to win her father's love. She'd tried, heaven knew, but he'd always found her irritating and she'd got in the way. Yet he needed her now and she couldn't let him down. And she did love Trader. Life without him was unthinkable.

Claire walked from the sun into the shade of the porch. She shivered apprehensively. Butterflies and gremlins were scurrying around her body, making her feel faint. She was afraid to go ahead with the wedding—and horror-struck at the idea of stopping it.

Silent and nervous, trying to find the right thing to do, she waited while her friend Sue adjusted the Southern-belle neckline and fussed with the huge puff sleeves so that the material lay in beguiling folds off the shoulder. Suddenly feeling very naked with so much creamy skin gleaming in the half-light, Claire twitched them up. They slid down again.

'Leave them!' teased Sue fondly. 'You're marrying a passionate man, you idiot, not a monk!'

'Passionate!' she repeated faintly.

Yes, he was. It lay in the darkness of his eyes, the intensity of his words and the hunger in his mouth. Violent emotions lay behind that courteous exterior. Phoenix had said, 'You'll have great sex, darling!' and had made her blush. It had been something she'd blocked out of her mind.

Claire shivered as terror gripped her slim body with its iron hand. Passion meant male lust, passion meant anger: the two things she was scared of facing. And she recoiled from the thought of animal lust and anger entering her life, because she'd seen her mother destroyed by both.

Yet Trader *had* controlled himself, for her sake. Her chin lifted decisively. She would marry Trader without protest and *make* it all come out well. Love conquered all. 'Love reforms Blackmailer'. Her hopes rose again. She *could* show him what love could do; how it could heal and soften even the most desperate of men, the most power-hungry person who walked God's earth. She winced. It was a tall order. Her mother hadn't had much success with her father to date.

But if she *could* succeed, she'd save her mother the inevitable shock. Claire grimly shut her mind to the memory of her mother's last angina attack. It had been frightening, terribly harrowing. If anything should happen to the woman who'd devoted her life to her...

'I'm ready, Jack,' she said to her father, and was proud of the way her voice remained steady despite her nerves.

'About time!' he grumbled, jerking her into motion.

The 'Bridal March' began, silencing her giggling bridesmaids. Claire glided into the body of the church in a soft, rich rustle of her huge skirts. At the top of the aisle, she paused, deathly white beneath the softly falling veil, her fingers digging hard into her father's sleeve.

Curious faces turned towards her. To her left, the lovely, homely faces of many of her Ballymare friends who were chattering excitedly, their affection reaching out and wrapping her in a welcome warmth. Many were from the hotel where she and her mother worked—and where she and Trader had met when he'd come to stay.

But to the right swirled an alien clutch of salon-smooth complexions, exclusive clothes, designer hats and discreetly wafting perfumes that denoted Trader's few guests. Her solemn eyes swept over them in astonishment because she'd never expected such affluence. But Phoenix had said Trader courted the rich, like her father used to. Did Trader also live beyond his means, toadying to the wealthy? She didn't know. God help her, she didn't know.

'By Jiminy, there's a few million pounds repre-
sented there!' gloated her father triumphantly in her
ear. 'Clever girl!'

'Jack!' Claire's cheeks burned with mortification.
One of Trader's guests had flinched at her father's
remark.

Miserably she walked at a funeral pace down the
long aisle, between the stunning displays of blue and
cream flowers that adorned each pew and which
drowned her in heavy perfume.

And finally she found the courage to look at Trader.
Seeing the heart-stopping spread of his broad back in
the beautifully tailored morning coat, she felt the
tension in her fingers miraculously ease. Slowly her
hand uncurled, longing to touch that neat, dark curve
of hair above his tanned neck and to relax the un-
natural stiffness of his head.

Oh, God, how she loved him! Her anguished eyes
burned into his back. If he'd turn round, she reasoned,
everything would be all right. Even at this eleventh
hour it would be a joy to find her worries wiped away.
She didn't want to hurt anyone today; not her mother,
her father, her friends, Trader . . . herself.

Turn, Trader! she pleaded. He must know she was
there! Her satin-clad feet were tapping on the grating,
her many petticoats were rustling. Everyone else was
looking! Didn't he care?

'Oh, Trader!' she breathed plaintively.

'Claire, darling!' whispered someone close by. With
a start, Claire recognised the warm tones of the woman
Trader had lived with for most of his life. Phoenix's
beautiful, exotic face swam into focus. 'You look ill!
Should you be here?'

Claire went limp with gratitude. Someone cared. 'No,' she husked. Her tongue flickered nervously over pale, dry lips and she gazed at the raven-haired Phoenix, pleading to be saved from her nightmare.

Before that could happen, her father's strong, expensively tanned hand reached out and patted hers and even he—insensitive to the condition of other people—could see that it was pale and trembling where it lay against the cascades of cream and pastel blue flowers that were appliquéd on to the fabric.

'Pull yourself together, sweetie!' he growled.

She *was* together. That was the trouble. Her rational mind had woken up and it was discovering all the flaws in her dream. Her love had been too unconditional, too trusting. She was an unsophisticated chambermaid. Trader was handsome and desirable.

Like her father! And *he'd* never been faithful...

Quite suddenly, Trader turned, jerking around with a sharp, impatient movement. She gave a small gasp of hope and her heart quickened its beat. But there was a frown instead of the usual look of adoration on his dark and handsome face; a frown that was replaced by a chilling stare as his eyes swung between her and her tense father. And the hatred between the two men blasted down the aisle with a shockingly tangible force.

'Oh, no!' she moaned, panicking.

Blindly, consumed by an unspeakable dismay, Claire tugged her hand from her father's arm and half-whirled around, hampered by the trailing material and the weight of the long, flower-strewn train. She would run! She'd get into her car, leave Ballymare and never come back!

CHAPTER TWO

CLAIRE heard murmurs of consternation from all around her as she gathered her skirts up for the dash to the door. Then her father caught her hand and jerked her roughly back to his side.

'You want to humiliate both your parents?' he hissed furiously.

'I want to be happy!' she whispered.

She rocked on her feet but managed to hold her ground. The murmurings grew louder while she stared in confusion at Trader, who looked equally alarmed, small beads of sweat glistening on his brow. Hopelessly muddled, she gripped her skirt convulsively, causing some of the petals from the flower swags to float to the floor.

'He loves me, he loves me not,' she intoned inaudibly to herself, superstitiously counting each petal as it fell. 'He loves me, he loves me not...' Her breath stopped. 'He loves me!'

Her lashes fluttered up in the unlikely hope that the childish game had some foundation. Incredibly, Trader was smiling gently and the love in his eyes made her give an involuntary sigh of bemused pleasure. She was totally oblivious to the chorus of sentimental sniffs to her left and the amused smiles to her right. Her father tugged in vain. She was transfixed. Immobile.

I love you! Trader mouthed, tenderly, adoringly. And she melted. Stupid she might be to go against every ounce of rational thought in her brain, but with that affirmation, all her worries vanished in a rush of relief and a shy delight.

I love you! she mouthed back in soft, heart-aching delight, seeing his whole body relax as though he'd been tense and uncertain too.

He loved her. She'd put her life on the line that he did. That heart-stopping worship in his soul-searching eyes couldn't possibly be faked!

Her slender body still trembled but now she glowed and her smile broke out, filling her face with radiance. She sighed in sheer relief at the narrowness of her escape from a life of misery without him. Seeing Trader's loving face, she *knew* there was more to the blackmail and Trader's strange behaviour than her father had let on. There must be another side to the story, and between them they'd work out a solution to living their lives decently.

Courage and confidence lifted her head on its slender neck. Like a graceful swan, released from its ugly duckling stage, she floated towards Trader, the man she loved, an incandescent joy on her face. And to her great delight he came slowly towards her as if he couldn't bear to wait any longer to be near her, to touch her. That was how she felt. They'd been apart for too long. Hours!

She was aware, briefly, of her mother's moist eyes and hugely happy smile beneath the ridiculous little hat Trader had helped her choose. It made her look young and beautiful, thought Claire fondly. And saw how quickly her mother transferred her gaze to her father, and ached at the intense longing in her mother's sweet face. Dear Ma! It took all sorts!

And Claire vowed to forget her father's jarring behaviour and questionable ethics and to concentrate on the fact that he had the power to make her mother content, after years of unhappiness. If they got together, her mother could give up work at last and her angina would be more manageable and less life-threatening. Claire smiled with joy.

'I hope she knows what she's doing!'

Claire flinched, but she didn't let Phoenix's anxious aside dim her smile at all. She did know. Trader was stretching out his hand to her and she had eyes only for him.

'My beautiful madonna,' he said softly.

Shivers chased down her spine at the way he looked at her. Nice shivers. They made her feel special. Cherished.

'Trader!' she husked.

Filled with a wonderful lightness of heart, she reached out and took his hand, watched him half disintegrate, saw the strong jaw working, the swallowing of a lump in his throat that echoed hers—and, unknown to her, almost everyone's in the church.

'Trader,' she sighed happily.

He loved her!

Firmly he drew her to his side and his fierce, possessive look told her that he never wanted to let her go again. Lovingly he guided her the last few yards down the aisle. And, elated beyond belief, she shyly lowered her eyes to quietly savour the wonderful moment of certainty. Her dreams were safe and love would conquer all their difficulties. Feeling the acuteness of his relief, she felt privileged and humble that she should have prompted such a profound love in a man's heart.

His hand tightened its grip a little. 'Claire!' It was a wonderfully husky growl that never failed to make her feel she was being caressed and it reached deep into her bones. 'You worried me for a moment back there!' he said softly. 'I thought that——' He gave a low laugh that still had an edge of relief to it. 'I thought you were going to jilt me!'

The clergyman fidgeted, the starched cassock crackling meaningfully, but Claire's eyes pleaded mutely for a moment to speak to Trader.

'If I had?' she asked gently.

'I would have caught you and kissed you till you surrendered to me,' Trader murmured. He smiled. 'I love you, Claire!' he said with fierce conviction. 'I love you so much it stops my breath!'

It was everything she'd wanted to hear. Shaken, she slowly lifted her lashes and he must have seen the pearly tears at the corner of her huge, soft eyes despite the folds of the gossamer veil, because he gave her a tender, understanding smile that brought a blinding happiness to her face.

The intense devotion in her expression, her unworldly beauty and his compellingly handsome profile, produced a ripple of wistful envy that ran through the church in a low murmur.

Her lips parted. But she couldn't speak for the lump in her slender throat and touched him on his broad chest instead, with a loving, worshipping hand. Which he took in his and kissed lightly before he turned to the moist-eyed cleric in front of them.

'Please go ahead. We're ready,' he said, with an authoritative nod.

And Claire felt the excitement mounting within her, a mist of love around her that little else permeated. Dimly in the background, she heard the organ notes die away and then the clergyman's gentle voice. 'Dearly beloved . . .'

Trader squeezed her hand rather hard. She tried to listen carefully to every word, every special phrase she and Trader had chosen from her mother's old prayer book, so that she could savour every second of her wedding-day—so nearly abandoned.

Now she understood her mother's unshakeable devotion. Once you'd experienced true love, you were never the same again. There was a painful, contradictory seesawing of feelings: a deep core of tranquillity and an adrenalin-spinning excitement. Elation and security. Irresistible drugs of the mind. Trader satisfied all her emotional needs. That was enough.

She stole a look at the man she loved: the clean sweep of brow, the aggressive nose and determined mouth, the achingly beautiful angle of cheek and jaw. An intensely masculine man. Potent, a little unnerving, mysterious.

Her knees weakened. He shot her a look, his eyes glittering with such a fierce excitement that it came close to . . . triumph.

'. . . not to be undertaken lightly or wantonly . . .'

Her body stiffened a little because her conscience troubled her over that. They were marrying with secrets between them. Maybe without a dowry Trader wouldn't give her a second thought. His hand squeezed hers reassuringly. In fact, his grip was so tight that she could feel the unusual dampness of his palms and the impression of her bones against his flesh.

'. . . but reverently, discreetly, advisedly . . .'

The pressure on her hand increased till she gasped and turned her huge green eyes to him in apprehension. It was as though Trader was afraid she'd take fright and run. Claire shrank into herself, alarmed by her suspicious thoughts.

Somehow she quelled her disloyal doubts and fixed her gaze on the solemn priest. Every word was of deep significance to her. Marriage was holy. Not to be undertaken lightly... There was a clatter behind them; one of Trader's guests had dropped something—a portable phone, by the sound of it. And he drew in a deep, harsh breath that filled his body with a rigid tension.

Stricken by her overwhelming misgivings, she steeled herself not to tremble.

'Therefore,' intoned the priest, 'if any man can show any just cause why they may not lawfully be joined together, let him now speak, or else hereafter for ever hold his peace.'

There was a stifled cry behind them which made them both jump. The vicar looked up in sudden alarm as a shocked hush fell. Trader stopped breathing and prickles went down the back of Claire's neck. Trader had tightened every muscle in his body as though he feared and anticipated a denouncement.

She felt her skin become clammy. And then she heard what she'd been dreading. A clear, ringing word that echoed accusingly in the silence...

'*Wait!*'

Claire gave a low, despairing moan of horror and fainted dead away.

It seemed but a moment before the darkness that surrounded her became murky. Voices impinged on her unconscious and slowly she recovered to full awareness—but she kept her eyes tightly shut because she couldn't bring herself to face anyone. The shame, the awful, hollowing disillusionment, rocketed through her, draining away all normal resilience.

And she tried to untangle her mind because she was no longer lying on the cold, stone floor of the church. It seemed she was sitting in an armchair; she could feel its welcome softness beneath her lifeless body.

Quite motionless, she began to gather the foggy facts together. There'd been an objection to their wedding. Her stomach did its sickening swoop. The whole scenario was so like *Jane-Eyre*! Trader must have a wife. In the attic? she wondered hysterically. What attic? Where? Perhaps *children*! Hordes of them! How dared he! She wanted to hide forever...

'I'm sorry, I'm sorry! You know I'd never hurt you——'

Claire all but stiffened at the pathetic whimper. It was Phoenix—Phoenix, when she wanted her mother's shoulder to cry on...

'For God's sake, shut up!' rasped Trader brutally, shockingly. 'I'm damned if I'm cancelling the marriage! It means too much to me!'

Claire barely stifled a groan of dismay at the giveaway remark and the extraordinary change in his character. He'd never been curt or angry before. Never rude. But then she'd never known the real man, had she?

'Face up to it, darling; she's either highly reluctant, or she's feeling ill. You can see she's in no fit state,' said Phoenix gently. 'She wasn't exactly galloping up the aisle.'

'She was very pale——' conceded Trader grimly.

'You noticed? Even under all the layers of make-up? I'm afraid it's possible she's discovered your plans,' said Phoenix, forgetting to whisper.

Of course, thought Claire. Phoenix would know everything. They'd been friends for so long. And last night Phoenix's conscience had prompted her to hint that Trader was being deceitful, even though her loyalty meant she couldn't openly betray him. Poor Phoenix—what a dilemma!

'Keep your voice down, for God's sake!' Trader growled irritably. 'Leave this to me! I can bring her round better on my own. You can make amends by going to Brodie—Claire's mother—and apologising on my behalf for ordering her out of here so rudely...say I was upset. Tell her Claire is fine. Make Brodie relax, or I'll have your hide!'

'Bully,' said Phoenix amiably.

'Fee, get the vicar to announce that Claire is recovering, ask everyone's indulgence for ten minutes and get the organist to play something cheerful,' Trader snapped, rapping out the orders like a man born to authority. Her father had ordered her mother around in a similar way, Claire remembered, appalled. '*Now get out!*' Trader finished forcefully.

'I don't like what you're doing——' protested Phoenix.

Trader made a warning sound in his throat that apparently made Phoenix scurry out in fear, because there was the click of high heels tapping on a flagstone floor and then a heavy wooden door slamming.

The full horror of her situation finally hit Claire. She'd fallen hopelessly in love with Trader, but to him she was nothing more than a potential goldmine, to be exploited and plundered at will. And if his behaviour with Phoenix was anything to go by, he'd push her around, given half a chance, and treat her with contempt. She knew what that did to a woman. Knew what damage a dominating brute of a man could do. And she wasn't suffering that kind of treatment.

'Claire?'

The pulses in her wrist began to beat a fast tattoo. Trader was bending over her, she sensed that from the movement of air in front of her and the delicious shiver down her spine. She felt her veil being lifted back and his soft breath on her painfully composed face. Her own breathing deepened, lifting her breasts high, despite her efforts to remain unaffected.

'Damn!' He reached around her, bringing her forward, and to her astonishment his fingers closed around her zip tag!

She gasped, hearing—feeling—the movement of the zip and the lessening of the pressure of her tight bodice. Cool air met her upthrust breasts as they spilled luxuriantly from the dainty strapless basque, her lashes fluttered open in alarm and she found herself staring directly into a pair of glittering black eyes, as dark and as dangerous as a slick of tar.

'Claire!' he whispered softly, sensually.

Petrified, she lifted her arms to cross defensively over the luxurious material of her bodice and her hands came to rest on the sumptuously perfumed swell of her creamy breasts. Trader's nostrils flared, his eyes lingering avidly on the rapid rise and fall of her delicately boned hands as they tried to slow her breathing by pressure alone.

'No! Don't *touch* me!' she gasped, shrinking back into the chair and he jerked back as if from a blow, straightening up with a muttered curse.

'Hell! What—?'

'How *dare* you do that? How dare you take the first opportunity you had to...? Oh! You're a brute!

A despicable, disgusting brute!' she whispered incoherently.

'My God!' he exclaimed, his face pinched with anger. 'You think...! Dammit, Claire—your dress was tight! I thought you needed air in your lungs, darling——'

'Don't *darling* me!' she cried in fury.

'Hey!' He frowned and gave her a little shake. 'Still groggy? This is me, Trader! How far did you think I was going to go? he demanded, sounding bitterly offended.

'That's what I want to know!' she muttered defiantly, her eyes fixed miserably on his.

The muscles in Trader's jaw tightened, the insult eating into every visible inch of him. 'Thanks for the vote of confidence,' he said tightly.

'Confidence?' she scathed. 'I'm to have confidence in you?'

'Ye gods! Where's the shrewish tongue come from?'

She didn't know. Claire flushed at the rebuke and frantically tried to lift her bodice back to cover the half-naked globes of her breasts. For a moment she thought she saw hunger flicker around his strained mouth, but it set back into hurt lines again and she knew he was going to deny any idea of assault.

'Where are we?' she asked frostily, hunting around for clues.

'The church vestry.' His wary eyes watched her as if she were a bomb that might go off at any minute. 'You've got a few minutes' grace to recover.'

'If I do,' she said wildly.

'Of course you will,' he soothed, a worrying edge to his voice.

She squirmed under the compelling glance, saw his gaze drop as if hypnotised by her quivering breasts and she froze. Beneath her fingers, she could feel the treacherous excitement firming each peak and knew that she was quivering from the frisson that always came when he was near.

There was a horrid silence between them as if they were adversaries in some ghastly Cold War. Desperately she tried to interpret his expression, to find something—anything—that told her he felt concern or a residue of love for her. But the dark, smoothly tanned face had become quite inscrutable. Her eyes glimmered with contempt. He didn't want to lose her—or rather the money that came with her. He'd want to coax her back to the altar, wouldn't he?

'I'm sorry. You must have had an awful shock,' he said with disarming gentleness. Almost disarming.

'Terrible,' she replied bluntly. 'I would like some water, please.'

'Of course. Forgive me, I wasn't thinking,' he said in stilted, courteous tones. He went to fill a glass from the small wash basin and she took the opportunity to struggle with the zip but her fingers made no headway. 'Let me,' he said politely, putting the glass on the table beside her.

'No! Don't touch me!' she snapped hastily.

'For God's sake, Claire! What the hell's got into you? I told you I was applying common sense and first aid! Do you think I'm an animal?' he growled.

'I don't know!' she wailed. Other than her father, what did she know of men? How they behaved?

'God!' he exploded angrily, balling his fists.

'Don't hit me!' she warned unsteadily.

His eyes flickered with a lightning flash of rage. He sucked in his breath and slowly released it before allowing himself to launch into a chilling reply. 'I'm not like your father,' he said coldly. 'I don't hit women. The rough treatment your mother had to suffer——'

'Don't you dare to speak of my father like that!' she flared defensively, shamed by his perception. 'You know nothing about his marriage!'

Trader seemed to be making an effort to control himself. It was like damming a river in full spate, she thought nervously. 'If you say so,' he said tightly. 'I regret the remark and I made it in temper. But I don't hit women, Claire. Whatever the provocation. Now listen. This is a church vestry. There are one hundred and fifty-two people, a vicar and a dozen choirboys a few yards away. Even if you think I'm the sort to jump on you at any given opportunity,' he continued sarcastically, 'you surely can't imagine that I'd choose this particular moment, when I've had ample opportunity before, on beaches, in cars and in secluded woods?'

Her face flamed at his listing of the times when she'd been achingly willing. 'No. Of course not. I believe you. I felt...vulnerable. Muddled.' She put a shaking hand to her head and looked at him in appeal. 'I feel terrible that—I—I reacted without thinking,' she said miserably, wishing her zip would come unstuck. 'I'm sorry.'

He grunted and watched her ineffectual wriggling with ill-concealed impatience. 'Why don't you give in?' he sighed. 'You'll never do that up on your own.'

'I—all right. Thank you,' she mumbled, wanting to cry.

'My poor darling,' he said huskily. 'You must be feeling awful. I hate to see you upset.'

And she wanted to believe that. But the lies seemed to come too easily to his lips, the adoration flowed too freely from his drowsy eyes. She had been vain to imagine she could have captured his heart when he was so handsome, so unnervingly sophisticated and worldly.

Oh, God! She blanched. Was that how her father had seduced his second wife into parting with her fortune? By charm and stealth and smooth talk?

Trader came to stand behind the chair, and remained there for several seconds without doing anything. The hairs rose on the back of her neck while she sat waiting, her hands firmly gripping the low neckline of her dress as a precaution. Eventually, after an eternity, he swept the headdress to one side in a drift of silk that caressed her smooth shoulder in a soft, erotic whisper and she gave an involuntary shiver. Her whole body waited for the touch of his hands and every fibre of her being had become focused on her naked and unprotected back.

'Claire——' he husked thickly.

'For heaven's sake, get on with it!' she cried in agitation, unable to bear the suspense. There was a sensation running down her spine that frightened her. Fear and anticipation. Half of her wanted him to kiss each vertebra, to surround it with his warm mouth. The rest of her wanted to pick up her skirts and run for safety. A snake-pit would be fine.

'Of course, darling,' he soothed and she felt the satin voice wash over her, calming her doubts despite her struggle to stay wary. 'We *are* pushed for time. I merely wanted to say how I adore you. How much I want to hold you in my arms.' He gave a wicked little chuckle. 'But it wouldn't stop there, would it?'

Yes, she wanted to say. It would.

One of his palms came into contact with her back and she shuddered again, the desire to have it stroke her skin far too strong for her to deny. But Trader grunted, she felt the tug on the zip and so she drew herself erect to help its slow progress upwards. It couldn't be that difficult a task, but she seemed suspended in a heavily dragging time while the material gradually closed over her lower back and then each straining rib; one by one, inch by excruciatingly exciting inch.

Probably to taunt her, he took a painful age to do up the fastening at the top, and she agonised over the touch of his fingers on her flesh. Something fierce and raw was piercing her body, something alarmingly sexual had made her vibrate to his practised caress. Each time he brushed her skin she quivered with a strange, vibrant life that made her blush with shame.

It was deliberate, she told herself. Part of his seduction. And mentally she clad herself in an impenetrable armour.

'It's a beautiful dress,' he murmured. Idly his hand ran down the sheathing material that now encased her back. 'You have such a tiny waist,' he mused, sounding huskier by the second. 'I think my hands could——'

'*Please*!' she breathed in agony. The armour was melting!

In a sudden, abrupt movement, he appeared by her side and wordlessly handed her the water. 'Tell me when you feel you can continue,' he said, his features as brittle as his voice. He regarded her with steady, unsmiling eyes. Cold, bleak, scary. It wasn't her imagination that tinged his words with a sinister menace. He was watching her warily, as though judging the extent of her surrender to his magnetic personality. 'Your mother will be worried,' he said quietly.

'Don't you think I know that?' she cried angrily. 'You don't have to rub it in. I hate the way you and my father use her condition to force me to do what you want!'

'I want to marry you,' he said tightly. 'That's hardly the vile deed you seem to be suggesting by your tone. I'm sorry if I pressurised you. But do me a favour and don't bracket me with your father in the same breath!'

'You're alike,' she muttered and met his glittering eyes with defiance.

'Not by one iota,' he said savagely.

Her eyes reflected her mute contradiction. Both were big men, both were charmers who liked to get their own way. And, now that she had to tell him she wasn't going back, what would he do? He was very physical—she knew that, from the way he'd run across Ballymare beach with her, while she perched on his shoulders. Strong, too; his hands had made light work of shifting Dan O'Connor's heavy old boat. She quivered with nerves.

But they couldn't begin married life with dark secrets between them. She loved him deeply and she didn't want him to marry her because she was attached to a pile of money. She'd rather wait till he came to her of his own free will. Her legs trembled. She sought to hide that fact by twisting them around each other beneath the huge skirt.

'I think you have something to tell me,' she said in a weird little croak.

Trader froze. He's guilty! she thought in dismay. Her hands began to shake visibly and she put the glass down, straining to interpret the expression on his bleak face.

'I have? Like...what?' he asked, non-committally.

'Let's start with why someone stopped our wedding ceremony!' she said quietly. And added, 'Or did that escape your notice?!'

'Hardly,' he said coldly. 'Nor did your sarcasm. I don't like your tone, Claire.'

Her eyes flashed. 'And I don't like your secrets!' she cried hysterically. 'Can't you see what a state I'm in? Just tell me and put me out of my misery: what exactly is the reason we shouldn't get married?'

Every stupid inch of her was screwed up in anticipation of his answer and she knew with a terrible despair that she was more than eager to believe *any* excuse he dreamed up. And how she'd loathe herself if she did! He had her heart and soul. It would be disastrous if he claimed her pride as well.

'None. I'm not married, I've not been certified insane and I have all the parts a woman could want in a husband. And I don't have any notifiable disease. OK?'

She flushed. 'Don't patronise me, Trader!' she snapped.

'I was trying to lighten you up,' he grated. 'You don't have a lot of faith in me, do you? God help us both if something *really* serious comes to test us,' he added thoughtfully. She glared but he went on, 'There was no objection to our marriage. Poor Phoenix was being hassled by some guy, wanting her address. She got irritable and told him to wait.'

'That's all?! It—it sounds far-fetched,' she said hesitantly.

'It's the truth!' he insisted. 'I was shaken too, Claire. I've been on edge ever since we parted yesterday afternoon. I haven't slept, wondering whether you'd turn up this morning——'

'Is there a reason I shouldn't?' she asked quickly.

He grimaced. 'A thousand. Or so I persuaded myself.' His mouth made a half-hearted attempt at a wry grin. 'I've never felt so unsure of someone in my life. Or as uncertain of anything. It's a new experience and I don't like it.' He ran a hand through his hair. 'I came here for a break in my hectic life, not to find a bride. I have things to do which don't leave room for a steady relationship, let alone a wife. But...you can't ignore opportunity, can you?' he said with a rueful grin.

'Maybe we both should,' she said bitterly.

'Look, I know I've pushed you for this marriage. But you know why.'

'Yes,' she said shakily. 'I think I do.'

With a groan, he knelt at her feet and laid a firm hand on her knee. Its heat burned through the layers of petticoats, warming her frozen skin. But despite his apparently submissive position, she had the impression of being trapped. His strength, his faint air of menace, the piercing command of his eyes all added up to domination. And she wanted parity.

'Thank God for that!' He gave her a dazzling grin that lit up his face and, fool that she was, she immediately felt that he was the man she'd fallen in love with again. 'Darling, all I want is to be with you,' he said persuasively. 'I know you feel the same. I don't need anyone else. You're my friend and always will be. Doesn't that tell you we have something special, something unique?'

Claire's thick fringe of lashes closed with the sweet memories. They'd been so happy walking hand in hand. Wandering in quiet companionship, needing nothing but each other. 'Oh, Trader!' she said tremulously, wishing, wishing for his love. 'I do love you! I do, I do, I *do*! I want to spend the rest of my life with you because you make me feel complete! And then I start to think of reasons we shouldn't be together, instead of listening to my blind instincts and——'

'Then stop thinking!' he ordered sternly. 'It's cracking us up! We need one another. It's that simple. Let's get married without any more of this damn fool talking!'

She sniffed as the tears of relief filled her huge, forest-green eyes. 'If you love me, truly love me, I'll marry you. I—I didn't want to be hurt, you see. I feel horribly defenceless where you're concerned and...my mother's experience has made me protect myself,' she sobbed, her body in convulsions of weeping.

And then Trader was peeling her fingers from his waist and gently holding her at arm's length while she stood weeping in front of him.

'I understand that,' he said quietly. 'It would be easy to hurt you. Once committed, you give your whole self in a relationship, holding nothing back. But you have to trust me. Say you will marry me now or I'll have to walk out of your life for ever.'

'That sounds like an ultimatum,' she said slowly, knuckling away the tears in surprise.

'It is. I'm not going through this again,' he replied, his dark eyes steady on hers. 'This could be our only chance of happiness. You see, darling, you're in a unique position to change my life.'

The money would change his life, she thought sadly. He'd be rich instead of poor. 'Trader——' she began, but his finger stopped her lips.

'If you doubt me, if you reject me now, I'm not hanging around for an encore.' The words were cold and uncompromising. He stood back and gave her a little shake, fixing her with his glittering stare. 'My father was a very proud man. So am I. It's difficult for me to admit that I love you so much that you could destroy me. But I'm taking the risk because I think it's worth it, you idiot! This is my final gamble,' he growled. 'Yes, or no?'

CHAPTER THREE

CLAIRE felt weak and tired from lack of sleep. Or perhaps it was more from the constant tension, the terrible demons that had tormented her since yesterday evening, followed by the drama of the morning. This wasn't the time to be making any lifetime decision but she wanted the fairy-tale and she wanted Trader. The happy ever after.

Her lips parted. He might be a bastard. Have a terrible past. She had no way of knowing. But if he left, she'd *never* know and she'd always wonder. The scales slid one way, hovered, and then tipped precariously in the opposite direction. He swore that he loved her and she believed him. Without him she was only half a person. She had no choice but to marry him, whatever the consequences, or she'd regret it for ever.

'Yes,' she whispered helplessly.

'Thank God!' he muttered and gave her a sudden grin. 'The condemned man lives again! I've been pronounced innocent of the crimes.' Claire smiled wanly. 'You look shattered. I'll get Phoenix to help repair your make-up——'

'No!' she protested. 'I want Sue——'

'Phoenix,' he insisted. 'I can trust her not to say anything. She has my best interests at heart. Remember, you felt ill. Lack of sleep, nerves... Your mother must never know about your doubts. I'll tell everyone you're on your way.'

He was through the door before she could insist. In a panic, she staggered to the small washbasin and peered at herself in the mirror above. Rivulets of tears had made inroads into the make-up that Sue had helped her with earlier in an attempt to liven up her wan face. She heard Trader talking to Phoenix and hastily rubbed her thumb to smudge make-up across the telltale tear-streaks.

'Hello, Claire,' said Phoenix warmly, coming over and giving her a hug. 'You poor little scrap! I'm sorry I gave you a fright. How wan you look—and no wonder! What awful things must have gone through your mind about this reprobate!' She exchanged a fond smile with Trader and turned back to Claire. 'Forgive me?' she asked, with a catch in her voice.

'Yes,' answered Claire huskily. 'It—it actually gave us some breathing space to talk things through.' Her face lifted to Phoenix's. 'I know he loves me now,' she said shyly.

'Of course you do!' cooed Phoenix. She found her compact and began sweeping a block powder over Claire's face. 'I'd better do your mascara,' Phoenix sighed. 'You're really not used to wearing make-up, are you?'

'She doesn't need it,' broke in Trader lovingly.

'Course she does!' scoffed Phoenix. 'She's got to do something to tone down that orange hair. Lord, Trader, you can't go around looking suave and sophisticated with a little Irish colleen in tow! Look up, Claire... You need lashings of mascara on those ginger lashes. Better!'

Phoenix smiled, unaware that her words had worried Claire. Close up, Phoenix was incredibly beautiful, her pale, alabaster skin flawless, her dark hair drawn back from her face to show its incredible bone-structure, the elegantly understated hat giving her an enviably confident air. This woman knew more about Trader than she did, thought Claire wryly.

'Leave her alone! I love my Irish colleen. I could eat her!' chuckled Trader happily. 'Come here!' Like a fool, she obeyed before she could think, detaching herself from Phoenix's detaining hand. Trader pulled her to his body. 'This is for the woman I love,' he murmured.

His mouth claimed hers in a gentle kiss. It disarmed her, persuading her to forget everything in her mind, obliterating everything, removing the armour completely. Her own lips flowered beneath his and she felt herself growing boneless in his arms.

'Trader!' complained Phoenix, close to her ear. 'You're ruining her lipstick, darling!'

He laughed exultantly, a fevered light in his eyes when they met Claire's bewildered, blinking gaze. Phoenix dabbed at his lips in a sisterly fashion and then clucked crossly over the smudge at the corner of Claire's mouth, trying to elbow Trader out of the way as she repaired the damage.

'Trader... It will be all right, won't it?' faltered Claire, too worried to be put off by Phoenix.

He smiled his tender smile and she was lost in the glittering depths of his eloquent eyes. 'You're very precious to me,' he said huskily.

Then, before she could respond—or even crush the treacherous thought that she had a very precious dowry, he was striding out into the church with her hand tucked in his, excitedly hauling her breathless body past a line of gaping choirboys, past her mother, who kissed her and sniffed away a tear or two, till she came to rest beside her worried-looking father again.

'Claire's fine. We're ready,' said Trader with a ringing satisfaction.

And the ceremony began again. Throughout, Claire felt a bittersweetness in her heart. All her life, she'd dreamed of this moment and now it had come, it wasn't as she'd imagined. Even Trader's loving glances didn't ease her ache, however hard she tried to tell herself that her love would be enough.

'You're very quiet,' he said gently, during the photographs afterwards.

'You do love me?' she blurted out, to her deep embarrassment. 'Hey, listen to me!' she joked uncomfortably. 'I sound like a whining wife already! I mean——'

He was laughing, the lines around his eyes and mouth creasing appealingly. 'You look up at me with that incredible sweet face, wearing that gorgeous dress filled with your glorious body and you ask me if I——'

'I mean *love*,' she said in reproach. 'Not physical attraction.'

'I hadn't finished. Sexual attraction is an important part of what I feel for you but it's not enough to make me rush into marriage.'

'What is?' she asked, her throat dry.

'Work it out,' he teased. 'I'm thirty-five and I've been around a bit. I've known many women and I've had a couple of serious affairs. Suddenly I decide to get married.' He bent and dropped a light kiss on her nose, smiling with a loving exasperation. 'Doesn't that tell you anything, idiot?' he asked affectionately.

'Not really. You could have married me for all kinds of reasons,' she hinted.

'I did—dammit, just *wait*, will you?' he yelled at the photographer, and everyone laughed when Trader took her in his arms and kissed her stiff mouth very thoroughly, softening it despite her determination not to be coaxed. 'I've married you because you're reserved, quiet, unassuming and tough,' he said huskily. His mouth claimed hers again. 'Because you're restful to be with and I feel as if I've known you all my life. Because we both like silence and remote places and these past few weeks have been the happiest of my life.'

'Really?' she asked hopefully.

'Really,' he murmured against her soft lips. 'It's been wonderful to find peace away from the hurly-burly of life and to be with you. I love you, Claire. Let that be engraved on your heart.'

Dizzily she let him peel her fingers from his chest and blushed as everyone clapped in delight at their sheepish faces. And she held his declaration in her heart and let it comfort her, vowing to think positively about their marriage.

He held her close on the way to the reception at the hotel and she felt content to be in his arms. As various people hugged and congratulated them, she knew her face was glowing with happiness—and so was his.

'Feel all right now?' he smiled, as they made their way to their seats at the table. 'Not worried you've married an ogre?'

'No!' She smiled back and wanted to explain. 'But you are a stranger to me and you can't blame me for wondering if I've done the right thing. All I know is that you drink your coffee black and strong, you never eat cake and you're crazy about sunsets!'

'Not a bad inventory. You also know I like crispy bacon and fried eggs for breakfast——'

'Nothing for lunch and that you have a passion for seafood and good wine,' she said slowly, arranging her dress with care as she sat down on the chair he held for her. She looked up at him thoughtfully. 'It's not much to go on, is it? Only a fool would get married knowing so little about someone!'

'But perhaps it's only fools who fall in love,' he said, smiling into her eyes. 'Common sense vanishes when your heart is committed to someone. Don't you think it's exciting to want to be with someone so badly that you'll risk putting your life in their hands?'

A shiver went up her spine and he must have seen her tremble, because he placed his warm hand on her cold one and massaged it gently.

'It's scary,' she said solemnly. 'I've never taken a risk before.'

'Look forward to our exploration of each other,' he said. 'You know we're right for each other. Look into my eyes and see the love I have for you. Look into your heart and read what's written there. You'll find my name.'

Claire relaxed and kissed him, overwhelmed by the strength of his love. She would trust him because she wanted to. And so she began to enjoy herself, letting her doubts recede and allowing her happiness to shine through.

It seemed that she floated on a cloud all through the meal and the speeches, even when her father rose to speak and Trader sat stiff and tense till he'd finished.

But the strain left his face when the dancing began and Claire was delighted to discover that he seemed reluctant to ever leave her side.

'People will talk!' Claire grinned happily, her eyes flirting with Trader as her partner was gently shouldered aside. 'I finish a dance and you material-ise from nowhere—if you haven't cut in on my partner already!'

'I don't want you talking to strange men,' he said smoothly.

She laughed as he took her in his arms. 'Well, *you're* a strange man—and I'm talking to *you*!' Her arms went around his neck. '*Luke*,' she said reproachfully. 'I married a Luke Benedict! You fraud! I thought I was getting a guy called Trader!'

He smiled a little thinly. 'Thank your lucky stars it wasn't Albert!' He nuzzled her cheek. 'If you were surprised,' he murmured, 'so was I. When the vicar told me to repeat, "I, Luke, take thee, Claire," I almost turned around to see who you'd got lined up in the queue behind me!'

Claire laughed delightedly. 'Then my father had a coughing fit and you scowled at him! Perhaps he thought you were someone else, too!'

'I think, for a minute, he did,' Trader murmured drily.

A balloon banged into her head. She turned around, laughing and saw Phoenix smiling at her so she batted the balloon back and Trader quickly whisked her away.

'To think I nearly walked out on you,' she said softly.

He kissed her cheek. 'You would have talked yourself out of an adventure. The adventure of our lives. What happened, Claire?' he asked casually. 'Bridal nerves?'

'It was the way you looked at me when I walked down the aisle,' she admitted. 'Angry and hostile. I was afraid——'

'Forgive me,' he sighed, his mouth drifting over hers, coaxing her lips to kiss him back. Small, delicate kisses. Comforting. Persuasive. 'I could see how nervous you were. I felt as if I was on the edge of a precipice. I wondered if... if anyone had been counselling you against our marriage——'

'Should they?' she asked, tensing inside.

Trader lifted his shoulders in an eloquent shrug. 'People interfere,' he said gravely. 'You were late and I was getting nervous. I willed you down that aisle, you know! You looked so forlorn and uncertain, I had a passionate urge to protect you.'

'How lovely!' No one had protected her for a long time. She'd always been in charge, caring for her mother when she came in tired from work, easing her mother's burden by running the house, from when she was nine years old. It would be wonderful to have someone look after her for a change.

'Hell! There's Phoenix making a beeline for us again! I wish we were alone,' frowned Trader. 'On honeymoon. Under blue skies and waving palm trees. Just you and I and——'

'The sand flies?' laughed Claire, her heart swooping at his smouldering eyes.

'No problem. I'll cover your body with mine,' he said huskily.

'Trader!' complained Phoenix, putting her hand on Trader's arm as the music stopped. 'Keep your smutty remarks to yourself!'

'That wasn't smutty,' he said softly, kissing Claire's smooth forehead. 'That's love. I doubt we'd notice the flies, anyway. We'll be too wrapped up in each other. As we are now. I doubt I'd notice if the world stopped turning, right at this moment.'

'Oh, Trader!' Deeply happy, Claire touched his face in a graceful gesture. 'You're very romantic——'

'Romantic? Trader?!' squawked Phoenix, inadvertently intruding into the dreamlike moment. 'So what romantic things has this reprobate done?'

Laughing at Phoenix's look of frank disbelief, Claire thought of the soft dark night when they'd first gone out together. They'd been blanketed by the velvet blackness and had bobbed about in a boat in the bay till the glory of the dawn had filled them with powerful emotions and he'd kissed her for the very first time.

'Taken me night-fishing,' she began huskily.

Phoenix lifted an amused eyebrow and clutched Trader, shaking him in mock reproach till his hold on Claire was broken. 'God! Trader! You'll have to do better than that! Fishing!'

'And we sat on a seat in the rain, under an umbrella,' said Claire softly, not in the least perturbed. Kissing. Tasting the rain on each other's faces, oblivious to everything but their love.

'Fishing? Rain!' Phoenix said weakly, her hand dramatically slammed to her forehead. 'What's come over you, Trader? What happened to those romantic dinners served on a polished walnut table with solid silver and crystal glasses set in a private room, the roses pinned to the walls, the blindfolded musicians playing——'

'Button your mouth, would you?' he murmured, his rolling eyes making a mockery of the dramatic description. But there was a slice of underlying steel in his tone. 'Claire appreciates the simple things in life.'

'Blindfold musicians would be nice,' she said with a grin.

'I'll order them on the first night of our honeymoon,' he told her solemnly.

Phoenix made a vomiting movement with her fingers and stalked off, swaying her seductive hips. Trader watched her for a while then his hands stole to Claire's uplifted ribcage and she drew in her breath, provoking his growl of appreciation as her breasts were thrust high above the scooped neckline.

'You're beautiful, Mrs Benedict,' he murmured, his eyes lingering on her translucent skin. 'I want us to go,' he said urgently. 'Now!'

A hot quiver ran through her entire body, wiping away the laughter on her face and giving her an unconsciously sultry look. 'We haven't been here long!' she protested huskily. 'Weddings go on for hours and hours. You're not doing me out of the fun, *Luke*.'

'Don't use that name!' He took the edge of his sharpness with a rather forced smile. 'I prefer Trader,' he explained winningly.

'Luke suits you. I like it—it's more friendly. Why did you change it?' she asked curiously.

'Why not? Let's go outside and smooch,' he suggested, propelling her into the garden.

Under the wistaria canopy, he kissed her till her head grew dizzy. Mindless, she slid her arms around his neck, unable to resist the feel of his silky hair over her fingers, the clean, fresh smell of his warm skin. And she allowed herself to be overcome by utter love, irrepressible joy. It came surging wildly through her in a huge sigh.

'I want to hear all about you as a little boy,' she said sentimentally, nuzzling deeper into his shoulder and kissing the line of his jaw. It tightened. He was grimacing as though his childhood wasn't pleasant. 'Did your parents call you Trader?' she asked curiously.

'No.' He hesitated and then said, 'It became my nickname when I was at school. I did a few deals.'

'Like what?' she coaxed, a little apprehensively. The name smacked of underhand salesmanship.

'Oh, this and that,' he said vaguely. 'Buying broken bikes, cannibalising the parts and selling them on as working machines again. You know the sort of thing.'

'It's not what you do now. You said you worked in a bank. I can't really see you as a teller,' she admitted. 'You're far too self-confident. It must be a city bank in Boston.'

'Yes. It is. I still get involved in complicated deals on the side,' he said casually. 'Bit of risk-taking. A little gamble now and then,' he added with a dismissive smile.

Her face fell as she remembered that she was one of his complicated deals. 'You gamble? Take risks with money?' she asked anxiously.

He gave her a hard stare, his thick black brows lowered in a heavy scowl. 'If I do, I think that's my business, don't you? Don't worry,' he said, an edge of icy reproof in his tone, 'there'll be enough to go round for you as well.'

She flinched. Her dowry would be more than adequate for them both if he didn't gamble it all away. And she wanted to give a large amount of it to her mother. 'Father gambles. He always did, even when he was a chauffeur and didn't have much money. And Mother suffered as a result. I never want to be as desperate as she was!' she said fervently, hoping he'd get the message.

'He's a bastard!' muttered Trader. 'Did he ever pay your mother any maintenance when they parted?'

Claire's eyes saddened. There was deep contempt in Trader's face and she felt the urge to remind him that he wasn't perfect either. 'No.'

'Yet he's as rich as Croesus!'

She bit her lip at the condemnatory tone. 'The woman he went to live with offered Mother a lump sum,' she said reluctantly. 'Mother refused. Please don't be hostile to Jack,' she begged. 'You're bound to upset Mother. It's her dream to be reunited with him.' Claire fell silent for a moment, knowing from Trader's grim expression that he didn't approve of that idea. 'I know, I know! It's crazy, but we shouldn't care about our own feelings about this,' she said passionately. 'Only that Mother is happy! I'd be more than content if she was just fit and well and financially secure for the rest of her life. She works too hard. I'd give anything to enable her to retire.'

'I understand,' he said softly, thoughtfully. 'It's a laudable ambition. And your dream?'

'To make her life easy,' she sighed.

Trader seemed very still. She shot him a glance and was pierced by his glittering eyes. 'She comes before me?' he queried flatly.

Claire flushed. 'I thought you meant as far as my mother was concerned,' she replied, feeling upset that she'd hurt him. 'Trader, she's had a hard time——'

'I know.' His face had become a hard mask. 'Your mother told me. Your father dumped her for a rich widow they'd both been working for. And she had to leave Jersey because she was in a tied cottage and couldn't cope with seeing her husband lording it in the very house she'd scrubbed and cleaned for most of her married life!'

Puzzled by his bitterness, Claire nodded. 'Mother doesn't tell people about Diana le Trebisonne,' she said in surprise. 'But you can appreciate why I want to do things for her.'

'And now you can,' he said softly. 'Your marriage has brought you money.'

She blinked. A dowry, for them to share. 'Yes. It has!' Her smile lit her face. 'I want to spoil her!' she cried eagerly. 'She deserves it, Trader! When she fled to Ireland, the aunts helped her out, but she hated taking their charity. She was pregnant with me when Father left her and she went without so that I had whatever I needed. She sacrificed things for me and that's why I want to help her and to look after her. You do understand, don't you? She shouldn't be working. I've been frantic lately. I'd do anything to stop her killing herself, inch by inch, day by day, doing that housekeeping job in the hotel! Is it any wonder I want to make her life easy, when she's been so un-selfish all her life?'

Trader cleared his throat. His eyes glittered and he seemed alarmingly angry. 'No,' he growled. 'But perhaps it's blinded you to the ethics involved in the choice you've made.'

'I don't understand what you mean. You'd do the same for your mother if she were still alive!' she said vehemently.

His expression became bleak. 'I think we should go back,' he said abruptly. He must have seen the film of moisture in Claire's eyes, because he sighed and held her close. 'I do care about your mother,' he said softly in her ear. 'I'm angry at the way your father treated her. When we're in Boston, she must come to visit and stay as long as she likes. We'll take care of her, Claire. We'll make sure she doesn't have to work again.'

'Oh, darling!' she cried, lifting her happy face to his. 'I'd love that!'

'Fine,' he said huskily. 'Now let's take advantage of that slow music, shall we?'

Claire was disappointed that the moment they began to dance, the dreamy music changed to something hot and fast. She laughed ruefully at Trader as he glared in the direction of the fiddler swaying away madly on his violin.

'Damn Phoenix!' muttered Trader. 'Why did she have to interfere?'

Her eyes followed his and she realised who had ordered the music to be changed. 'I expect she thought the party needed livening up.' She smiled ruefully. 'Loads more people are on the dance floor now.'

'Go with the flow!' he grinned.

With a sudden burst of elation, he swung her into his arms and whirled her around so fast that the balloons and banners became a blur of blue and gold and white, the extravagant candelabra and chandeliers bathing Trader's face with bronze lights. Her heart turned over as he stared into her eyes, compelling her to love him, hypnotising her into a state of total adoration.

People around them began to whoop in glee and their movements became more restricted as the dance-floor seethed with gyrating bodies. Soon they were forced to slow down to a more demure pace.

'I'm breathless!' she cried happily, her face aglow with exertion and joy.

'Wait till I kiss you. You'll know what breathless is!' he murmured.

A scarlet-clad arm came between them. 'Trader! Trader!' cried Phoenix, grabbing his lapel urgently.

'Don't be a bore, Fee,' he groaned. 'You can't cut in——'

'Phone call,' said Phoenix firmly, with a roll of her eyes at Claire. 'Does he think I'd want to *dance* with him?' she cried, sharing her mock horror with Claire and the two women giggled.

'Telephone? For me? Are you joking?!' he protested. 'Whoever it is, tell them I'm flirting madly with a married woman and don't want to be disturbed. I refuse to do business——'

'It's not that kind of call.' Phoenix angled her glossy black head and put her scarlet lips close to Trader's ear. Claire stepped back politely.

'Damn!' cursed Trader. 'Darling——'

'It's all right,' smiled Claire. 'You go ahead. I'll talk to mother and the aunts. I want to check Mum's OK.'

'Won't be long.' He kissed her nose. 'Don't run away!' he admonished and she grinned. 'If I catch you with a man, I'll flatten him!'

'Bully!' laughed Claire.

'Treat 'em rough and tell 'em nothing, that's my style,' he growled, and before Claire could become alarmed by that he kissed her slowly on the lips. 'Re-

member—stay with your mother and your aunts. I'll
expect to see you with them. Wait there for me...
No talking to anyone else!'

'Oh, God! You two! This way,' urged Phoenix.

Claire watched them go, thinking what marvellous
colouring Phoenix had: that white skin, her smooth,
black hair twisted into a soignée knot, scarlet outfit,
lips and nails. Very dramatic. She herself must look
very pallid in comparison. Phoenix had tucked her
arm in Trader's and they walked very close together,
in the way of old friends. It was very nice to see.

'I'd watch that woman, if I were you.'

Claire spun around, surprised by her father's
warning. 'Heavens, Jack! You've got it wrong!' she
said with a dismissive laugh. 'Phoenix is the sister of
Trader's best man, Charles. Trader's lived with the
Fairchilds since he was a teenager. They're virtually
related.'

'Fancy. Know why he lived with them?' mused Jack
idly.

'No. He never told me but I suppose it was when
his parents died,' she replied. 'He and Charles were
best friends at school. Wasn't that nice of the
Fairchilds to take him in? Pity they couldn't be here.
They're in Australia, I believe, and couldn't make it
back.' She watched Trader open the flap of the
marquee for Phoenix and place an affectionate arm
around the woman's waist. 'Phoenix was only a kid
when Trader came to live with them permanently and
she's idolised him ever since,' she added warmly. 'It's
lovely to be part of a loving family.' She bit her lip
and blushed at her lack of tact. 'I meant——'

'Yeah. Well, you've got your mother,' her father
drawled cynically. 'Trader's got Phoenix.'

'I'm not jealous,' she said gently. 'He does love me, Jack.'

'Sure.' He patted her shoulder awkwardly. 'Don't expect me to love *him*.'

Claire sighed. It would be a long time before she could ease the tensions there. She had a lot of work to do to mediate between everyone. Glancing up, she saw a look that resembled affection on her father's face and her eyes lit up. Hope at last.

Her hand touched his cheek tentatively and he didn't shrug it off, but looked bashful instead. So she kissed him and gave him a hug, that was briefly returned till he pushed her away with a gruff, 'Bloody weddings! Sentimental clap-trap!' And he marched off. But in his body she identified not anger, but a suppressed love, and she ran to her mother, her delicate face radiant with happiness.

It was quite a while later when her mother commented, 'Trader's a long time! I hope nothing's wrong.'

Claire suddenly stopped laughing when she saw the time on her new watch. She fingered the diamonds set on the bracelet and calmed her ridiculous fear. 'Maybe he's done a runner!' she joked, naming that fear and hoping she could laugh it away.

'Silly!' giggled her mother. 'He's been glued to you ever since you met! And he's not allowed anyone to spend longer than a few minutes with you today. Do you think he's entangled in some complicated business problem?'

'Fee told me he was a workaholic,' Claire said with a wry smile. 'I hope he hasn't forgotten it's his wedding-day!'

'There he is!' exclaimed her mother. 'Go to him, darling. He looks frazzled.'

'So does poor Fee!' grinned Claire, surprised at Phoenix's faintly dishevelled appearance. 'I hadn't realised she'd been dragged off to act as his secretary, or whatever! She looks dreadfully harassed.'

Happily she ran to Trader and flung herself into his arms. When he was slow to respond to her delighted hug—his reaction seeming almost desultory, in fact—she leaned back and wagged her finger at him.

'You've forgotten me?' she teased. 'Your bride?'

'Of course not.'

That was less than enthusiastic. Puzzled, she turned to appeal to Phoenix, but she'd been claimed for a dance and all she could see was the long, elegant body swaying seductively in her father's arms.

'Trouble?' she asked Trader sympathetically.

His dark eyes were inscrutable. It was a long while before he answered. 'Of sorts. It's been dealt with.'

'Phoenix actually looks harassed and untidy!' she said shakily. 'What—what did you do to her?' She'd meant it as a joke. It came out as an accusation.

'She got in a paddy,' he said curtly. 'She thought I hadn't paid enough attention to her—or the guests.'

That was true. As her mother had said, he'd been by her side almost constantly. 'Poor Phoenix. You must make it up to her. She's busy now. How about a dance with me?' she asked sombrely. He'd withdrawn from her. His moods were difficult to understand—and she did want to understand him, desperately.

'I'd rather not, if you don't mind.' He managed a smile but it was rather weak and didn't touch his eyes. 'I need some fresh air. I'll be OK in a moment. A rather unpleasant call, nothing more. I'm going for a walk. Alone. Would you check the arrangements with your mother, about coming over to Boston next month? I'll see you in a little while.'

The kiss felt impersonal; his lips were cold. Claire watched him leave, a heavy feeling in her heart. Something worrying had happened to change his mood and she had to ask Phoenix what that was. Anxiously she waited till her father relinquished his partner and then she hurried to head Phoenix off because she seemed to be heading for the marquee exit after Trader.

'Phoenix! Wait! I need to talk to you!' she cried breathlessly.

'Something wrong, darling?' The two dark brows winged delicately upwards.

'Here.' Claire drew Phoenix into a private corner behind an enormous display of delphiniums and lilies. The scent lay heavily in the air; rich, slightly sickly and a little funereal. 'Trader's acting oddly,' she said with total frankness. 'If he's in trouble——'

Phoenix took Claire's hands, met her eyes and then looked away, a little embarrassed. 'Well ... it's ... oh, I can't tell you!'

'Please!' begged Claire. 'Help me!'

'You poor kid,' sighed Phoenix. 'You poor, poor kid.' And she stroked Claire's hand sympathetically.

'Why? Why am I a poor kid?' croaked Claire.

The woman's eyes were pained. 'Nothing. I'm sure I'm being silly,' she said hesitantly. 'You're such a sweetie, he can't hurt you. I'm sure he can't——'

'Another woman.' Having leapt to that irrational conclusion, Claire gripped Phoenix's fingers till she was forced to meet her eyes and, to Claire's horror,

she gave a reluctant nod. The b
Claire's world. 'The phone call?'
his ex-lovers rang him?'

Phoenix drew in a long, slow breath
was Christabel.' She paused as though th
significant.

'Christabel who?'

'He hasn't told you?' Phoenix groaned. 'Da
He's known this woman a long time. They were
the brink of getting married. Look, Claire——'

'Please go on,' she said quietly, her face carved in
marble. Inside, it felt as if her bones were screaming.
How far had it gone? 'Did he love her a lot? Does
he . . . *still*?'

'Lord no!' Phoenix paused and Claire let out a huge
sigh of relief. But her next words weren't so welcome.
'That's why she jilted him at the altar.'

Claire's heart slammed in her chest with the shock.
No wonder he'd been nervous when she'd looked like
doing the same! 'Why did she jilt him?' she asked
shakily, when she'd found her voice again.

'Because Chrissie was an heiress,' explained
Phoenix. 'And Trader was marrying her for
her money.'

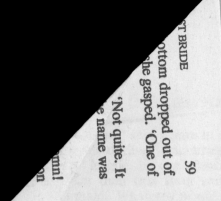

ottom dropped out of

he gasped. 'One of

'Not quite. It

e name was

...mn!

...on

...choked little voice. ...d Phoenix. 'You're ...chosen you for any- ...he? You're only a ...e gain by marrying ...women and living ...their backs are behind him, I'm glad to say. He's made a wonderful choice in you.'

Apparently Phoenix didn't know *all* of Trader's secrets, Claire thought bitterly. 'Are you suggesting he makes a habit of being a parasite?' she asked grimly.

'In the *past*, darling! God, he was so money-grabbing and calculating about women once!' she groaned. 'He really thought he could marry for money and make his way to the altar and unimaginable wealth by chatting up some defenceless woman! I was so delighted when I saw you,' she confided. 'You're so ordinary!'

'Thanks,' said Claire drily.

'Well, it must be love that's drawn him to you,' soothed Phoenix. 'You're not glamorous like the women he's fancied in the past and you're not rich and ugly like the ones he proposed to.'

'Oh, my God!' mumbled Claire.

'I think Chrissie rang to make sure Trader wasn't trying to deceive another heiress,' continued Phoenix. 'He put her right, of course. Though it took all his charm to persuade her not to come and check for herself! She was talking about turning up at the airport to meet you. He went mad when he hung up. It took ages to calm him down. It was almost as though he was scared stiff you and she would get together!'

Somehow Claire held on to her sanity. 'He didn't love this woman, you said,' she repeated woodenly.

'No. She discovered just in time that he was madly in love with——!' Phoenix clapped a hand to her mouth. 'Oh, God! My big mouth! Scrub that,' she said hastily. 'I didn't mean to say it!'

White-lipped, Claire challenged the remark with eyes as fierce and as dark as storm-tossed seas. 'I'm not stupid. It's quite obvious! Trader was hoping to marry this Chrissie because she was an heiress—and all the while he loved another woman! That's right, isn't it?' she demanded miserably.

'You sad little scrap! I hoped you'd never find out! And now it's too late! But he must love you. Hold on to that. The rest is old news. Don't raise the matter with Trader,' Phoenix begged. 'He'll never speak to me again if he knew I'd told you. And I couldn't bear that.'

Claire's lip quivered and it was a second or two before she could control it. 'This . . . woman he *really* loved. Is he . . . ?' She gulped. 'Is he still in love with her?'

'He *was* deeply in love for years and years, I can't deny that. He must be over her, now he's chosen you, mustn't he? Women come, women go—you know the kind of thing.'

She didn't. 'I can guess,' she said unhappily, wondering how many women had come and gone. And when she'd be added to that list.

'Claire,' said Phoenix smoothly, 'I overheard Trader saying that he's recently acquired a large amount of liquid funds and property. Lord knows how. Some questionable deal, I expect. He and I talked and...I'll tell you one thing; he's doing some very dodgy things with this money he's acquired. I don't think he means to share it with you, so don't raise your hopes. Still,' she added brightly, 'you're used to doing without, aren't you?'

So that was it. Trader was frittering away her father's money on some risky scheme. It would be wasted and his expansive offer to care for her mother might never be possible. She ground her teeth in anger.

And, she wondered, when Phoenix had kissed her, given her a sisterly, sympathetic hug and wandered off, how soon would it be before Trader had extracted all he wanted from his goldmine bride and went off to find a wealthier wife? Oh, Trader, she thought unhappily. I've risked my happiness by marrying you!

He loved her, he loved her not. She wanted to rip all the flower petals from her dress and rely on the superstition. It seemed that it might be marginally more trustworthy than her own feelings.

'Claire.'

'What?' She jumped, her mind whirling with her thoughts and found that Trader was standing in front of her, looking solemn and rather drawn.

'I think we should go,' he said curtly. 'Where's Phoenix?'

'Trader,' she said, plucking up the courage to say something. 'I—I want to stay. I don't w-want——!'

'No. Now!'

Ruthlessly he ignored her mumbled, stuttering protests and dragged her unwillingly to where Phoenix was tossing down one glass of champagne after another. 'We're going in a moment, Fee,' he said with a warmth and gentleness he hadn't shown to Claire.

While the stricken Claire remained stunned and numb, Phoenix gave him a shaky smile. 'Back with your wife at last, you rat?' she said lightly.

Feeling she was in a nightmare and watching the tragedy of her life being played out from the sidelines, Claire saw Phoenix tug at Trader's lapels in playful reproach. She felt a jerk of envy at the woman's lovely profile and the perfect curve of her neck.

'I am. And I have a couple of things to clear up before I go, Fee.' Trader met Phoenix's limpid eyes and it seemed to Claire that he looked at his friend with a deep understanding. 'Come on, sweetheart,' he coaxed. 'Dance with me before we leave.'

'Sure. Just a sec.' Phoenix discarded her jacket to reveal a strapless sequined basque and a remarkable cleavage.

Trader cleared his throat. 'Ye Gods! That's stunning!'

'Versace,' said Phoenix, brightening. 'You always love my Versace stuff.'

'Eye-popping,' he agreed drily. 'Don't mind, do you, Claire?'

She shook her head, her mind dulled and leaden. But she did mind. Jealousy had been woken in her—perhaps because she felt so uncertain of herself again. It seemed she was even envious of his childhood friend, stupid though that was.

Although she kept remonstrating with herself for such irrational feelings, it pained her to see their closeness. Not only in the way they danced: breast to breast, thigh to thigh, Phoenix's hands laced behind Trader's head, their eyes locked like lovers; but also how they talked and talked, serious, engrossed, riveted by one another.

Fee whispered in his ear. He whispered back, his mouth inches away, once brushing Fee's jaw when she turned her head unexpectedly. Every time he leant back, it was obvious that he would be getting an eyeful of cleavage. Not that he did that too often. Most of the time he was clamped so tightly to her that the sequins must be leaving pressure marks through to the bone.

It hurt. The whole of her body hurt. Claire ate a pastry that tasted like cardboard and tried to quell the growing sense of unease about Phoenix. They were old friends, she told herself. Childhood friends. And now they seemed to be arguing, as old friends did sometimes.

Her mind still raced with jealous demons, however. She was thinking that there had been two major relationships in Trader's life: Christabel—a woman he'd never loved and who'd jilted him at the altar—and a woman he'd loved deeply. That was no big deal. What sexy, desirable man hadn't flexed his passions?

Besides, she thought to herself, he'd married *her*, hadn't he? And then more demons came to taunt her. Two words that kept hammering in her head. 'Heiress'. 'Ambition'. And she tried her best to replace them with 'love', 'faith' and 'hope'.

'Striking woman.'

She jumped, and smiled weakly at someone who'd been introduced as one of her father's newest business acquaintances. 'Yes. She is. She's the most beautiful woman in the room,' she agreed without rancour.

'Almost. But not quite. You are,' the silver-haired man said with apparent sincerity. He smiled at her look of disbelief. 'I'll tell you why. Your radiance, your love for Trader, has made us all moist-eyed and envious, my dear.' He laughed when she blushed. 'I've seen your husband somewhere. I'm trying to decide where. You—er—you don't know if he has relatives in Jersey, do you?' he went on casually.

'My husband?' She bit her lip. The word had meant everything to her a short while ago. Now... 'Sorry,' she said, seeing the man's amused smile. 'Woolgathering. My *father* lived in Jersey once, but I don't know about Trader. I'm sure he would have said.' For a moment she hesitated, remembering that odd idea she'd had that Trader and her mother had known each other before. But Trader was too young; her mother had left Jersey over twenty years ago. 'To be honest, I don't know. I haven't got around to all the details of Trader's background,' she added with an apologetic shrug.

'I used to live there. I thought I'd seen him around. Could have been somewhere else, I suppose. But the face is very familiar... Oh, well. I'm getting old! Here's to your health and happiness, my dear.' The man lifted his glass to her and wandered off.

Trader was already coming across the floor towards her, leading a reluctant Phoenix rapidly through the dancing couples. When they were closer, Claire could see that Phoenix had lost some of her sparkle and fire and she wondered if their late night was catching up with her.

'Are you all right, Fee?' Claire asked sympathetically. 'You look tired——'

'I'm sad. What do you expect? You're taking away my dearest friend. We've spent a lot of time in each other's company over the last few months,' said Phoenix dully. 'I'll miss him. Dreadfully.'

'You'll be OK,' Trader said, his voice a little husky. And he gave Phoenix an affectionate smile. 'I'll be in touch while we're away. You know that.'

Claire blinked in surprise. She'd known they were close friends, but to phone Phoenix during their honeymoon? From the Seychelles?

Something cold settled in her stomach as they stood in front of her, holding hands, Phoenix looking as if her world was ending, her fingers entwined intimately in his, Trader's dark eyes unfathomable. She felt like an outsider.

Phoenix laughed in a rather brittle way. 'Don't leave without making up our quarrel!' she begged. And explained to Claire, 'We've had a row about what he's going to do with a load of money he's——'

'Shut it, Fee,' growled Trader. 'I'll do what I choose. I always have.'

Her father's money, thought Claire, feeling suddenly tired as she intercepted Trader's warning scowl at Fee. She gave an inward sigh. It wouldn't be easy, persuading Trader not to gamble whatever remained. But she consoled herself by promising that she'd do her best. And things would be different between them soon. Please God that they'd be different.

With a quick, hard glance to Phoenix, he said, 'We're off. It's a long flight. Check the Rolls is ready, Fee. Ask the driver to make sure there's nothing stuffed into the exhaust or the engine.' When she hesitated, he jerked his head, a rather fierce glint in his eye. 'Move it, Fee,' he said softly, giving her a playful shove in the small of her back.

'You won't be able to push Claire around the way you do me,' Phoenix said wagging a finger at him. 'No bullying, Trader. Don't act the bastard at *home*.'

Claire tensed. That suggested he was a bastard at work. 'Treat 'em rough, tell 'em nothing.' She watched the wiggling red hips sidle away and prayed that Trader didn't have her father's temper. She'd hated the way her mother had been dominated by brute force and a powerful, flawed personality. Claire's heart gave a quick somersault at the thought of leaving home for the first time with the unpredictable Trader.

'Can't we stay a little longer?' she asked hopefully. 'You've hardly given me time to talk to your friends——'

'They're enjoying themselves well enough without us. Let's sneak away,' he said quickly. 'You'll meet up with them often in the future. Plenty of time.'

'But I wanted to dig the dirt about you,' she teased, speaking without thinking. To her surprise, he tensed. It was only an imperceptible movement but she was so tuned into his body that she knew he'd become wary. 'I imagine,' she burbled, trying to sound cheerful and cover up her gaffe, 'you've dug out all my skeletons and it's time I unearthed a few of yours. I know you and Mother have been having a heart-to-heart. Did she tell you all my sins?'

'Oh, yes,' he said lightly, his face totally unreadable. 'I was informed that you're a grouch in the mornings.'

He looked over to where her mother stood. Their eyes met and he smiled. Claire wondered if her imagination was working overtime. If she didn't know better, she'd have said that it was definitely the surreptitious kind of smile that characterised a shared experience and knowledge. How odd.

'Well, there you are!' she declared, dismissing her irrational theory. 'You know my secret vice. What's yours?'

'Tenacity.'

'That's not a vice!' she exclaimed.

'It is, the way I hang on,' he said grimly. 'But at this moment it's impatience.' He smiled, a little stiffly. 'Now stop making excuses. We're going to change,' he said in a determined tone, and guided her to the door.

They were stopped several times on the way. To her dismay, she began to suspect his reasons for staying so close to her. Every time any of his friends began to extend the conversation to more than a platitude or two, he butted in and hustled her off. In fact, now she came to think of it, she'd never settled into a chat with any of his friends at all.

Trader had interrupted all of those attempted conversations with friendly banter of his own and smoothly changed the subject if his friends began to make references about his lifestyle. Other than the time he'd gone off with Phoenix for that phone call, and brief dances they'd had with other people, he'd been with her, monitoring everything that the guests said. She'd found that touching. Though now she realised that it had meant that he'd stopped his friends from saying anything incriminating.

Not once had she danced more than a handful of steps with anyone else before he'd claimed her; charmingly, persuasively, looking little-boy-helpless, as though he knew he was being unreasonable, but simply couldn't stay away from her a moment longer.

And she dared not ask herself why he was behaving like that.

Claire felt her hands going clammy as they came closer and closer to the suite, afraid of the sudden intimacy of removing her dress in front of... She gulped. A stranger. 'I want to change in a room of my own,' she demanded hastily.

'Whatever you want.' His tone was flat and controlled, as if he didn't care what she did now. 'I'll use my old bedroom. I'll wait for you here.'

But in the event, she was the one who did the waiting. In her new beige suit, she paced up and down, trying to hold on to her determination to offer such special love to Trader that he'd realise what riches he had gained.

When he finally appeared, he looked drawn and pale and her heart lurched in anguish. So she went up to him and kissed him lovingly, and it seemed that he melted a little before he pushed her gently away.

'Time for our goodbyes,' he said softly, and led her down the stairs again where the bridesmaids ambushed him, smothering his face in pink lipstick till they were elbowed aside by a determined-looking Phoenix.

'Darling! How can you go?' wailed Phoenix, flinging herself into his arms.

Subdued, Claire clung to his hand and waited while they kissed. Friends, making up after a quarrel. She nodded and forced herself to smile at everyone's good wishes, ducking in the vain hope of escaping some of the confetti showers, and wondering what Phoenix was now whispering in his ear.

Trader impatiently withdrew his hand from hers. He was frowning, now holding Phoenix as though he couldn't bear to let her go, and Claire tried not to envy their friendship too much, because it was understandable because they'd spent so much time together and they'd feel a little strange at parting.

'I expect,' said Charles Fairchild in a kindly voice, as Trader talked quietly and seriously to Fee, 'they're making last-minute arrangements. Come on, Trader!' he complained. 'Stop thinking about work and pay some attention to your bride!'

Claire burned with humiliation. Trader stayed his best man, said something which made Phoenix cry. Then he kissed her affectionately on both cheeks and tenderly wiped away Phoenix's tears.

'Trader!' protested Claire finally, tugging at his sleeve.

'She's upset,' he said quietly. 'That matters to me.'

More than your wife? she wanted to say petulantly. Then Claire became surrounded by her rosy-cheeked bridesmaids, all wishing her well and telling her how lucky she was. Over Sue's shoulder, she saw Trader watching her friends with a cynical expression as they half jokingly berated her for marrying a man who was sweeping her off to enjoy the 'high life' in Boston.

'I'm going because Trader lives there and because I love him,' she protested, because even she could hear the real envy in her friends' voices.

'Yes, sure,' teased Sue. 'Pull the other one! You only married him because he's got more money than you!'

'Claire knows what the score is,' defended Phoenix generously, and Claire flashed her a grateful glance. 'She knows Trader's worth. It's a girl's right to know things like that. Ask him for diamonds tonight, darling!'

She blushed. 'I already have a lovely watch and necklace,' she said awkwardly. And she sensed Trader's irritation in the abrupt way his hand came to lodge under her elbow.

'Let's go,' he said curtly, bundling her into the car.

The happiest day of her life, she thought bitterly. And he was just as unhappy. Was he regretting his marriage of convenience? 'Trader——' she began hesitantly.

'Wave to your mother, Claire!' he muttered irritably. 'She'll miss you dreadfully.'

'Wave to Phoenix,' she countered quietly. 'She won't know what to do with herself for two weeks.'

'What the hell do you mean by that?' he demanded, giving her a cold stare.

Claire blinked. 'Nothing! But she's crying and I imagine it'll be odd for her, not having you around——'

'Leave it,' he said tersely. 'We're going. Smile and wave.'

She became aware of the hands, banging on the window to capture her attention, and made herself lean forward so that she could see her mother. The car drew away slowly.

'Bye, bye!' Claire continued waving through the back window. The movement of her hand became more frantic. She felt afraid to leave her mother and her friends and begin a new life with a man who was becoming more and more of a stranger with every hour. Boston would be very different. A new culture, a new life, a new husband; so many adjustments. 'Bye!' she repeated softly, almost with a sob.

Her slim body twisted awkwardly as she strained for a last wistful glimpse before the huge fuchsia hedge on the corner of the road blocked her view. And then she slowly turned, shedding confetti with every move, and settled herself nervously in the comfortable leather seat, smoothing her beige skirt as they drove out of the small town.

Trader seemed very quiet. She stole a look at him and wondered if his remote expression was caused by the same uncertainties that were making her so apprehensive. Perhaps he was thinking of Christabel. Or the woman he'd once loved so desperately.

What were the two of them going to do over the next couple of weeks—let alone the following months? Remain in polite silence? She had to break the ice.

'It's not easy, starting a new life, is it?' she said hesitantly.

'No.'

Disconcerted by his monosyllabic response, she watched the hedges and fields sail by at a worrying rate and felt more homesick every second. Perhaps he ought to know that.

'I—I feel a bit upset, Trader.'

'Why?' His frown beetled his brows together.

Move, she begged with her eyes. Hold me. Tell me everything's fine, that you love me. *Me*.

'Well,' she said instead, with a nervous laugh. 'For a start, I've lived in Ballymare all my life. You know what it's like. It's a small, intimate community where everyone knows everyone else and all their business.' She paused. That sounded like a tourist brochure! she thought. Stilted. Awkward.

'You'll like Boston.'

'Oh, yes. Everyone says its lovely,' she replied politely, trying to be positive. But in Ballymare, it was safe to walk at night and no one worried because you weren't in the latest fashion and that you didn't know who Turnbull and Asser were. Colour invaded her face when she remembered Phoenix's shriek of appalled laughter when she'd helpfully told Claire what shirts he liked and his collar size. But how was she to know the name of a shirt maker?

Claire sighed. It would be harder for her to settle to married life because she was the one making all the changes. Trader was taking her to a remote island in the Indian Ocean, thousands of miles away, when she'd never left Ireland before. And then to his Boston apartment.

Wanting to hold on to a little bit of 'home', she clung to the memories of her lovely wedding and with the music and the dancing and the laughter of her dear friends still ringing in her ears.

Music, dancing, laughter... and the sight of Trader, kissing Phoenix a long goodbye. Her fists balled and she tried not to mind.

'At last the wedding's over,' muttered Trader.

She winced and turned her huge eyes on him. 'Didn't you like it?' she asked shakily.

He hesitated, then gathered her in his arms as if it were a duty. 'I didn't like sharing you,' he said gruffly. 'I hated you being with anyone but me. I hated leaving you for a moment.'

Grim-faced, he toyed with her hair, twisting a strand of disarranged amber around his finger like a silken ribbon, while she wondered if that was true. But once there *had* been love in his eyes, in his voice, in the happiness they had together—of that she'd been certain.

She mustn't, couldn't let her fears shake her will to make the marriage work. Whatever the reasons, however driven Trader was by the hunger for financial gain, they had got on well together. And their love would be stronger when they came through their troubles, when they'd talked things through. It was up to her.

'That's lovely,' she said, with some genuine warmth. 'But you did like meeting my friends, I know. And they liked you enormously.'

'Yes.'

The memory was so good that she smiled, took courage and snuggled into him, feeling a warm glow of pleasure steal over her tense body. 'It was a truly Irish wedding,' she sighed, trying to forget all her apprehension. They would sort their differences out and clear up any misunderstandings. She knew they would. 'It was nice to see everyone mingling and enjoying themselves,' she said happily. 'From those cute toddlers to old Mrs O'Hennessey.'

Trader gave a short laugh. 'My God! Could she dance me off my feet!'

Claire laughed and nuzzled up to his cheek, glad of a chance to ease the atmosphere. 'A real old family "do". I did enjoy it. You were a great hit,' she said, feeling pleased that her friends had found him so congenial. 'I thought your guests and mine would never mix. I'm surprised they did. Yours were so ultra-towny and sophisticated and mine must have seemed very unworldly,' she admitted.

'Chalk and cheese? People who are at the top of their profession don't have many hang-ups,' he replied casually. 'It's the ones who are hacking their way up you have to watch out for. They'll sell their souls to get what they want.'

'Would you sell yours?' As soon as she'd said that, she could have bitten her tongue out. And she realised how tense he was. With her body against his, she could feel his heart thudding madly against her side.

He paused. 'There are one or two things I feel very strongly about,' he said eventually. 'I think we'd all be tempted to sell our souls in some circumstances——'

'I wouldn't!' she declared with a small pout. 'Never!'

Trader grunted. 'What conviction!' he drawled cynically, his eyes a little mocking as he looked down on her. 'Every emotion and vice known to man is inside each and every one of us. Push someone too far, threaten what they value most, and the knives come out. It's a question of raw survival, Claire. I understand it well and I think you do, too. You have strong passions and fierce loyalties.'

'But I wouldn't sell my soul——'

'We both know you would,' he said softly.

Insulted, she lifted her hands from where they had rested against his chest and when she pushed herself away, he did nothing to stop her. 'You're judging people by yourself,' she said, feeling hurt. 'I'm not a sinner and never will be——'

'We can all delude ourselves on that point. It depends where you draw the line between sin and reprehensible behaviour. When the Devil tempts,' he said sardonically, flipping open his silver-grey jacket with a casual gesture, 'it takes a strong person to resist. I know that goes for me, on those occasions when I've been slammed up against a wall with nowhere to go but forward. I advance with all guns blazing and mow down my enemies.'

'You do?' She didn't like the way he was talking and she let her distaste show.

'Sure. And I'll get around to telling you about that some day. For now, I'm bushed. One dance too many. And now we're married. A few weeks ago I didn't even know you. Fate springs some odd surprises. How do you feel now we've tied the knot, Mrs Benedict?' he asked, peering at her, his eyes a little wary.

'Odd,' she admitted quietly. Fate had been surprising her, too. 'A bit disorientated.'

'Let me orientate you, then.'

Without easing his implacable expression, he bent his head to kiss her lips but she recoiled from the scarlet imprint across his mouth that had come from his clinch with Phoenix. Seeing his quick frown, she forced a smile.

'Have you seen your face?' she asked hastily, wagging a reproving finger. 'You look like a lipstick advert!' she told him with wincingly jolly cheerfulness.

He touched his face with a wry twist of his mouth. 'I thought those women would eat me!' he grimaced. 'Clean me up, will you? Use this.'

Oblivious to her reluctance, he reached for the bottle of champagne that was sitting in a bucket of ice in front of them and opened it with an expert and gentle pressure, pouring some into a glass and moistening his neatly laundered linen handkerchief. Obediently she rubbed at the smears that marred his beautiful skin till they vanished. There was only the slash of red across his lips to tackle.

'It won't come off,' she said with a frown after a moment or two.

'Kiss it off,' he suggested, challenging her with a long, slow glance from under his thick lashes.

'No! I won't!' she blurted out, stiffening her whole body as he pulled her closer. 'I don't want to——'

'What?' he asked, quietly alert.

'I—I don't want to kiss you——'

Trader's eyes flickered and his hands dropped from her arms. 'How interesting,' he said with quiet menace. 'I was warned you might not.'

Claire's eyes rounded. 'Warned?' She frowned. 'Who by?'

'Fee,' he answered surprisingly. 'She thought you looked rather sullen at my lack of attention to you when were saying our goodbyes. She told me to make allowances if you played hard to get in order to teach me a lesson.' His lip curled in contempt and his eyes mocked her bewildered expression. 'How very innocent you look,' he drawled. 'Are you going to kiss me, or not?'

She kept her eyes glued to the great expanse of his shirt-front. 'Not with another woman's lipstick all over your mouth.' Her chin lifted and she looked him directly in the eyes.

'Another...? God, that's only Phoenix!' he said irritably, yet he touched his mouth thoughtfully.

It was a significant gesture that wasn't lost on her. 'Only?' Her voice shook and she fought to steady it, trying desperately to pull the awkward conversation back to normality. 'She's a very important part of your life, I think.'

He grunted. 'Vital. My right arm. She's quite brilliant. She trained as a lawyer and I find her invaluable. Without her, I'd be lost.'

Terrible scourging waves of jealousy rolled through her. Phoenix was so very lovely; always immaculately dressed, her make-up perfect, her nails beautifully shaped and her hands soft as silk. She was warm and caring, loyal, amusing, terribly sophisticated . . . and clever. Oh, and indispensable.

'I wonder you didn't marry her!' she said in an unnaturally high voice. *Fool*! she upbraided herself. Querulous, whining fool!

'I might have done. I asked her once,' he admitted, pouring champagne for them both and handing her a glass. His mouth closed over the wafer thin rim and he sipped thoughtfully.

And Claire's spine went rigid. Another woman in his life! Once he must have been in love with Phoenix, who had kindly protected her from that knowledge—and the head count was rising by the hour!

'Really?' she croaked in dismay, gulping the rather flat champagne. 'Good grief, this stuff has an instant effect on my vocal cords!' she said quickly, to explain away her weird voice. 'Whatever did she say?' Her pulses drummed fiercely in her temples as she leaned back and tried to behave casually.

He smiled faintly, remembering. 'She said "not till you're rich, darling!" She'll be rich in her own right one day——'

'I know.' Claire tried not to dwell on the fact that he had now met Phoenix's terms. 'She told me when we were chatting last night,' she said with more false brightness. 'She inherits from her father's trust providing she doesn't get married till she's thirty.'

'Poor Fee,' said Trader sympathetically. 'Her father ensured that the trust reverts to Oxfam if she marries earlier than that. She's got five years to go.'

'She's so beautiful. Men would wait for her. Wealth and beauty combined is a mixture that'll tempt a lot of opportunists!' declared Claire, meeting his eyes in a reckless challenge.

His mouth twisted. 'That's why she vowed to marry a millionaire. And when I knew that,' he said, 'it motivated me to make a fortune.'

'But... you married me——' she ventured shakily.

His burst of laughter cut her short and his eyebrow lifted in a secretive, amused arc. 'I think you will turn out to *be* my fortune,' he said surprisingly, and so glibly too, that she winced. 'And I yours.'

Claire frowned. 'What?'

'Several people have commented on your good fortune——'

'*My* good fortune?!' she exclaimed indignantly.

Trader leant back and negligently crossed one elegantly clad leg over the other. 'Sure. You become wealthy by marrying me.'

'Yes,' she acknowledged, 'that's very true,' and said boldly, 'And since you have a tendency to gamble, I think I should control the purse-strings for both our sakes.'

There was a deathly silence. Trader fixed her with a glacial stare. 'Over my dead body,' he said softly. 'You really are a greedy little cat, aren't you?'

CHAPTER FIVE

FOR a moment, Claire was speechless, quite stunned by his vicious outburst. And deeply wounded. A man in love didn't say things like that. 'I'm not a cat!' she said angrily, a tremor in her voice as she tried to stop herself from bursting into tears.

Her mind reeled with the implications. He meant to keep her short of money and make her go without, just as her father had done with her mother!

'You don't deny the greedy,' he commented laconically.

'I have a right to share——!' she began heatedly.

'Like hell you have! You're disgustingly like your father, aren't you?' he said coldly, shocking her because he'd made the same odious comparison with her father that she'd made about him. 'Both of you are corrupted by greed!'

'That's not true!' she cried, blushing because she was defending the indefensible.

'You're a liar. He almost bust a gut in excitement when he saw my wealthy friends in church!' Trader said scathingly. His gaze challenged hers and she blanched because she knew immediately what he meant.

'Dad was only kidding around——' she said huffily.

Trader's eyes gleamed. 'By gloating that you were a clever girl? I don't think so.'

Claire squirmed. 'It was only an idle comment! Your friend didn't have to repeat it! We were rather surprised that your guests looked so wealthy because you'd always seemed hard up,' she muttered reluctantly, wishing he didn't have the ability to compel her to be so horribly honest. Her lashes dropped to hide her embarrassment and she gave a small shrug as if it hadn't meant anything.

'Come clean. You weren't surprised at all,' he said flatly.

'I was!' she insisted. 'I expected your friends to be ordinary, like mine. After all, you only ever wore old clothes and——'

'But good ones.'

'I—I didn't know that!' she said impatiently, knowing differently since her chat with Phoenix. 'To me, they were just much-worn jumpers and shirts and jeans——'

'I think you know the makers of my shirt,' he said, interrupting her coldly.

'Yes, I do!' she agreed. 'Turnbull and Asser. But——'

He smiled grimly. 'The ties I've worn?'

She hadn't known anything about his clothes, till Phoenix had told her during the hen party, but now she did and she could see his point because he did dress expensively. 'Armani—but I didn't——'

'Shoes?'

'OK, I know they're Gucci, but——'

'I rest my case,' he drawled.

'I didn't know before last night!' she snapped resentfully. 'Phoenix gave me a list of your favourite stuff.'

'Even if that were true, you must have wondered how I could spend out on designer labels,' he pointed out.

'Some men do put all their money on their backs,' she defended. 'Father did. He was a dandy even before he——'

'Married money,' Trader drawled.

Claire took a deep breath. 'This has to stop, Trader! It's ridiculous! I was far too busy last night thinking about our wedding to worry about what you spent on clothes! Please don't let's bicker,' she begged. 'I regret Father's remark but he loves rich people. He's still like a kid in a toy shop. And you can't blame me for *his* snobbish comment. Good or bad, he's my father. I'd rather you said nothing at all than you came out with unpleasant remarks about him and insulted me,' she said unhappily.

'He ought to curb public displays of his naked greed,' growled Trader brutally. 'Like bragging about his mansion in Florida and the manor house on Jersey! I've never heard such a self-glorifying speech at a wedding in my whole life!'

Claire looked up at him sharply, her gentle eyes swimming with dismay at the intense hatred in his tone. 'He's proud of his success,' she said sullenly. And found it incongruous that she should be defending her father to her husband again. 'Especially the manor.'

'And is he proud of the way he acquired it?' Trader asked through his teeth. 'Charming a lonely widow, and leaping from chauffeur to owner via the besotted woman's bed? Bingo! Instant wealth, without raising an ounce of sweat! What nerve he had!'

'He was poor and struggling. I don't condone what he did but his head must have been turned at the thought of marrying Diana le Trebisonne, and dazzled to be living in a medieval manor house,' she said in a low tone.

Her long fingers fidgeted nervously on her lap. Her mother had loved the beautiful mellow stone manor house where she'd worked, and had talked about it a lot. Every detail had been described and exclaimed over a thousand times; the possessions cherished only by those who cleaned them, the gardens beloved by the staff, and the white sand beach where lonely Diana le Trebisonne had walked every evening, watching the sun set and coming home in tears.

Because her father had never been faithful.

'Poor, struggling and dazzled.' Trader's eyes mocked hers. 'That makes it all right, then.'

Claire went pink, irritated that he seemed determined to misunderstand her. 'Diana did love Father——' she defended.

'And because of that, she was blind to his motives,' Trader growled savagely.

'Yes,' she said miserably, identifying with the woman's helplessness.

'It's ironic,' said Trader cynically. 'Both your father and her first husband married Diana for her money.'

'What? Father and Philippe le Trebisonne, you mean?' she cried in astonishment. 'I didn't know *that*!'

'Common knowledge,' he said in a detached tone. But she could still hear the grim undercurrent. 'The Trebisonnes were bankrupt and the manor house was falling into disrepair. Philippe had to find himself an heiress fast.'

Claire blinked. '*Diana* was an heiress?!' She stifled a gasp. There were huge gaps in her knowledge that her aunts had taken for granted! And her eyes narrowed. Three men, Philippe, her father and Trader, had all chosen to wed money. She grimaced. Neat. 'So it was Diana who'd inherited the Fit for Life fitness centres?'

'And a vast sheep station in Australia and some Louisiana oil wells. So the predators swooped. Marriages of convenience seem unnervingly common nowadays, don't they?' he drawled and his eyes flickered when her mouth curled in scorn. 'At least Philippe was doing it for all the right reasons. He didn't want the money for himself, but to preserve a dynasty. After all, the Trebisonne family was threatened with extinction. The continuation of a dynastic family that's been in existence for five, six hundred years is a matter of great consequence.'

Trader's quiet, solemn tone stilled her for a moment and she had the odd feeling that he was identifying with Philippe and sharing in his dilemma. Two materialistic men out of the same mould, she thought, an icy sensation clawing its way up her back.

'Poor Diana,' she said quietly.

'Diana had what she wanted,' he said curtly. 'Position and prestige as a le Trebisonne. Marrying Philippe gave her entry into Jersey society when it would normally have been closed to the nouveau riche.'

'She didn't have Philippe's love,' she muttered.

'No.' His voice hardened. 'You can't have it all, Claire! There are people who would sell their souls to marry into a glamorous dynasty. A *rich* dynasty would be irresistible, wouldn't it?' he queried, watching her with narrowed eyes.

She searched his austere face and quailed. 'Yes,' she agreed quietly, and saw him flinch. One day the

Jersey house would be hers. And therefore Trader's.
He might have sold his soul to marry into a rich
dynasty. Despair filled her heart because she'd never
untangle his motives for marrying her.

'No one could be blamed for choosing to marry if
it got them out of the poverty trap, could they?' he
asked softly. '*Could they*?'

Claire cringed at the violence behind those two
words. He wanted her to justify what he'd done—and
she wouldn't. 'But you couldn't spend a lifetime with
someone on that basis!' she declared tremulously.

'You're damn right you can't!' he muttered.

Suddenly, Claire knew for sure that he'd never intended to stay married to her longer than absolutely
necessary. A terrible wave of nausea rolled through
her body and she leant back, waiting for it to pass.
But a cold sweat had broken out on her face and,
seeing it, Trader reached in his pocket, dabbing at her
forehead and neck with a terrible mockery in his cold
black eyes.

She let her lashes flutter down because she couldn't
cope with his intense dislike. History seemed to be
repeating itself. The Jardine women—Diana, her
mother, herself—had all been used by heartless men
who'd traded on their weakness for falling in love with
bastards.

Although her mother had said nothing about
Diana's personal life, Claire remembered how unhappy her mother had been, the deep insecurity that
had permeated her whole life, the feeling that she was
worthless because her husband hadn't desired her.

It was something she had to face. Now. She needed
to know what her marriage promised before they went
any further. 'It—it would be hard to make love to

someone you saw as a meal ticket,' she probed hesitantly.

'Depends on how much you needed sex,' he growled, and his eyes lashed hers with a bitter contempt.

Unnerved by his answer, she crossed her legs and knew his hungry eyes were scanning them so she pulled her skirt down where it had ridden up to her silk-clad thighs with the sudden movement. Too late. His breathing had stepped up its pace and depth.

'Claire,' he growled, 'come and kiss me.'

'No, Trader!' she protested. She needed time. Time to teach him love... His mouth tightened in determination and she wriggled away. 'Remember the driver!' she cried in panic.

'Over here,' he husked, roughly pulling her into the corner so that she lay half across his body, 'and with the privacy screen down,' he added mockingly, with a swift closing of the opaque shutter, 'he can't see a thing.'

Trapped and vulnerable, she pushed at his body ineffectually, desperate not to be treated as a sex object. 'My suit will get creased!' she mumbled.

'To hell with your suit!' he complained, his mouth only inches from hers. 'To hell with everything. I need to feel your mouth on mine. Kiss me! Let's forget the things that divide us and remember what we both need. Sex. The pleasure of touching one another.' His eyes became drowsy, firing her body with a liquid ache. 'God, Claire,' he murmured, 'you're turning me on!'

'I—I'll look like a dishrag at the airport——' she objected, somehow keeping herself stiff and unyielding. Her body arched back and she did her best to avoid his tempting, searching mouth that had so recently kissed the beautiful Phoenix.

'So that's really how you're going to play it, is it?' he murmured, and she wasn't sure if he was teasing or really edgy. 'You'll torment me, keep me at arm's length till we're in the bridal suite! And then ... what will you ask for? Baubles? Presents? Cruel woman!'

'Please, Trader!' she breathed hoarsely.

Gently his finger traced her jawline and slid to her throat. 'And you're tense,' he drawled, lifting her, despite her struggles, so that she lay completely across his body, her head on his breast. And she listened to the loud thudding of his heart as he talked to her soothingly and stroked her elaborately coiffed hair. 'Why is that?'

'It's been a tense kind of day!' she dissembled wildly, knowing that she was weakening with every skilful caress of his maddening fingers.

'I suppose it has, for both of us. We don't know what to make of each other yet. But I'll get your measure.' He gave a low and regretful laugh. 'We should have eloped. Got married in jumper and jeans. No hassle, no nerves, quick and painless. Quickly to bed in a small Irish cottage with a peat fire burning away,' he said softly, pulling out one of her hairpins.

'Don't!' He was trying to sweet-talk her round! She shot a hand up to stop him and he firmly took it away.

'I've wanted to release this coiled fire for hours,' he muttered, kissing her forehead and throwing hairpins in all directions.

'You didn't like it swept up?' she said, all muffled by his warm, beautifully firm chest. And angry that she felt irrationally pleased. She hadn't liked the new style, either.

'It's too glorious for that.' She could feel it tumbling into his hands now, and he spent a long time in silence, curving his palms over her scalp, seemingly enjoying the sensation of warm silken hair beneath his fingers. 'Too lovely to be forced into obedience by pins and lacquer,' he mused softly. 'Fire and flame and golden sun, all rolled into one.'

He buried his nose in the fragrant strands and nuzzled his way around to her neck. Claire lay in a pained bliss, adoring his touch. And then she felt his hand slip between them and the release of a button on her summer suit jacket. And another—

'No!' she cried in agitation, managing to wriggle away. She sat staring at him warily, a great curtain of shining amber hair sliding to conceal half her face. He looked annoyed, but heart-achingly handsome, his own hair tousled and boyish and she felt such an agonizing lurch of love for him that it prompted her to hastily button herself up again in sheer protection of her vulnerable heart.

It would be too easy to lose her virginity in the back of the car! And that wasn't romantic. Or decent—and he'd know she could effortlessly be twisted around his finger. Her life would be a misery.

'Cold witch. Have some more champagne,' he drawled. And he slid her easily to the seat beside him. His features were masked now, concealing whatever he thought of her reluctance to let him explore her body.

A little cynical in the way he eyed her when she thrust out her glass, he gave them both a refill and up-ended the bottle in the ice-bucket.

'Cheers,' she said feebly, desperate to break the chilly silence.

'To my self-control,' he drawled. 'I hope it stands the test.'

Claire went a bright red. 'I—I'm not used to—to——'

'I know.' He drained the flute. There was a little moisture from the champagne on his mouth and he slid out the tip of his tongue to savour it, his dark, smouldering eyes hot and drowsy beneath the thick fringe of lashes. 'It's to my advantage.'

She knew that only too well! 'It'll be a little while before I adjust,' she said hesitantly, unable to tear her eyes away from his desirable mouth.

'Don't take too long,' he said thickly. 'I'm aching with need, Claire. And we have a long flight ahead of us when we get to Heathrow. I'll be climbing the wall by then. Having you constantly by my side, looking so provocative——'

'I'm not!' Her indignant hand clapped to her perfectly proper camisole top beneath the matching neat beige suit.

'It's not what you wear,' he said wryly. 'It's the way you wear it.' His gaze slowly absorbed her, inch by melting inch. 'You have a tantalisingly voluptuous body, under those clothes. Did you know that?'

She gulped. 'Voluptuous?' she repeated stupidly. Embarrassed, she shook her head, denying the storm raging inside her. 'I don't want to be that!'

He smiled in contemplation, evidently not believing her. 'We'll see,' he husked. 'I have ways of making you behave as wantonly as I like. Ways that will release a woman's inhibitions. Till she discovers the pleasure of her own body and what it's like to hold nothing back.'

It sounded like a threat, as if he had plans for a wild orgy in mind! Claire quailed. He expected a pleasurable sexual experience. She didn't know how to give him one. Not one that would match up to his knowledge of other, more worldly women. And he'd be disappointed in her failure, her total ignorance.

'Trader,' she croaked. 'Let's get this clear. Don't expect anything . . . of me——'

He'd stiffened, his eyes narrowing like a cat's. 'What do you mean?' he asked warily. 'What the hell do you mean by that?'

Her ragged breath hissed through her parted lips. 'In—in bed . . .' And she couldn't go on. The thought of being naked, of Trader's wicked black eyes examining her body and comparing it to other women he'd known, was too awful to contemplate. Or the thought of the physical act itself, without the love she longed for in his heart.

'You calculating little tramp!' he said with a soft savagery.

Claire gasped in dismay, convinced beyond any doubt that she had to protect herself from being a doormat. Sex would make her his slave. She lifted a stubborn chin. 'You can't expect me to—to——'

'I want it all,' he growled, his eyes clashing with hers.

'I can't . . . give . . .' Her croaking voice faltered and failed. She pressed an icy hand to her forehead. This was a nightmare.

Surrender to Trader would mean relinquishing not only her inhibitions, but her last, nervously guarded defence against being hurt. It was like jumping off a cliff. There was no going back. Once that final barrier had been broken, Trader would possess her totally.

Giving herself meant that she would be at his mercy, so vulnerable, so susceptible to being hurt by him, that she felt curls of fear tightening her stomach muscles at the very thought. He would have all the power and she would have none. She knew enough of that situation to know how damaging that could be to both parties.

Deeply alarmed, she bent her head and once again fumbled with the bracelet strap of the beautiful gold and diamond watch he'd bought her for a wedding present. Around her slender neck there was a gold and diamond necklace too, sitting heavily on her delicate bones.

'It was expensive,' he said in a hard voice.

'I guessed. Far too extravagant,' she retorted miserably.

She'd given *him* some silver seal cuff links to remind him of the seals they'd watched in Bantry bay. They'd taken up most of her savings and he'd shown a touching delight in them. But her watch and bracelet were worth a few thousand—so Phoenix had said!— and she'd ached that her father's money was being spent so quickly.

'Worth every penny,' he said coldly.

Uncharitably she wondered if the ruby bracelet he'd given Phoenix had been worth every penny too. Claire felt uncomfortable about ostentation and needless extravagance, and even more uncomfortable with her souring jealousy. Yet Trader *had* spent a small fortune—and to what end? Whenever she'd checked the time by her watch, she'd been reminded that this was probably part of her father's first hush-money payment to Trader. She stared at the pretty diamond second hand and watched her life ticking away and her misery made her reckless.

'You really think so? I suppose you're expecting a handsome return on your investment?' she muttered huffily.

'By God! What have I married?' he wondered under his breath. Claire gave a low moan of shame and he caught her wrist in a ruthless grip. 'Damn you!' he roared. 'What's the matter? Look at me. *Look at me!*' he ordered, jerking her chin up with a quick thrust of his thumb and forefinger.

She met his malevolent eyes and felt fear crawling inside her stomach. 'Don't bully me! I don't like being hauled around like a doll you own!' she cried in panic as his shoulders lifted with anger. 'I won't be thrown in the corner of a car and subjected to a mauling I don't welcome!'

Trader's brows met in a deep scowl. 'I hope for your sake that your reluctance is only due to temporary nerves,' he said in a low rasp. 'We're both tired, jumpy. We have both sacrificed——' He clamped his mouth shut as if he'd said too much.

'What have you sacrificed?' she breathed. There was a tenfold increase in her pulse rate. She was hoping he wouldn't admit that he'd sacrificed his chance of marriage to the woman he loved.

'My integrity, among other things, by the looks of it,' he muttered.

'Your *integrity*!' she repeated incredulously. He flushed and she knew that he'd taken her meaning; that she was surprised he knew the meaning of the word. 'You talk of integrity, when you held my father to ransom?'

There was a cold silence. 'My God! She was right! He told you...*everything*?' he asked flatly.

Her world stood still, her mind occupied solely with the fact that everything would now come out in the open. 'Yes. He told me everything,' she said bitterly. She waited. 'Nothing to say? No explanation or excuses?' she demanded jerkily.

'No,' he said harshly. He leaned back, eyes like black stones and stared savagely ahead. 'You went into this with your eyes open, then! You're admitting that you knew what it would mean to be party to a cold-blooded marriage.'

It was true! Claire felt the tears start to her eyes. 'I—I tried to block out the motive but I can't. It affects the way I feel——'

'Tough. Our marriage wasn't arranged for you to sign your name on a bit of paper and run,' he said angrily. 'If you were implying a moment ago that you didn't want us to become lovers, I have news for you.' His hand touched her thigh and closed around it like a vice. 'This marriage is going to be consummated. As soon as we get within hailing distance of a bed. Or even before that, if there's the slightest opportunity. Perhaps I shouldn't wait at all. I'm tempted to assert my rights—*now*. Here in the back of this car, whether you like being mauled around or not.' Long fingers explored, inching higher up her thigh and Claire could feel the heat and the hunger pouring out of him.

The raw, sexual threat in Trader's voice robbed her of speech. Trapped by his bruising fingers, she couldn't hide the dismay in her enormous, liquid green eyes as the shock waves from his intense masculinity battered on her fragile defences.

She'd picked up a final, brutally telling phrase, 'Our marriage wasn't *arranged*'... All too clearly it dawned on her that he'd condemned himself completely; freely, casually admitting the disgusting pact he'd made so that he could lay his hands on some easy money. She had all the proof that she'd been as good as sold, bartered for her father's salvation and Trader's ambition. And Trader wanted sex as part of that arrangement. He could whistle, she thought furiously.

'Would you force me to have sex with you?' she asked coldly, despising his crude lust for power, for money and the convenience of her body.

Contempt slithered across his eyes too, the sharp flick of his glance blistering her with its hostility. 'Would I have to?'

'Oh, I think you would!' she retorted bitterly.

'I'm that desirable?' he asked, his lifted eyebrow emphasising the sarcasm. 'Thanks for letting me know where I stand.' With a slow and insulting look, he studied her body. 'You're going to take some seducing, aren't you?'

She felt so overwhelmed with misery at the cold, loveless words, that she couldn't—dared not—answer at first. Instead she stared mutely at him till he gave a muttered exclamation and let her go. Immediately she was free, she scuttled to the opposite corner of the seat. Husbands couldn't force wives. It was against the law.

'You, seduce me?' she scorned, when she'd found her voice. 'Don't waste your time!' she said defiantly.

Trader swore viciously under his breath. 'I'll be damned! You're calmly admitting that you never meant to honour your vows, said in church not a few hours ago! Hell, woman, you and your father are as devious and as two-timing and as slippery as each other! We made a deal——'

'You made it! You and him! Not me! I want no part in it!' she yelled, suddenly angry.

'You little whore!' he snarled. 'I can't believe you could be so hard! All sweetness and light and soft, melting eyes! What were you dreaming of?' He thrust his hand into his inside pocket and brought out his wallet, peeling off twenty-pound notes and showering them all over her, and tears sprang into her eyes, making them glisten. 'These? Do *they* make your eyes light up? Oh, yes, I see the glint in them now.' In an insulting gesture, he held a note to her ear and rustled it. 'Listen. The lovely sound of money. Smell it,' he grated, thrusting it under her nose. 'The smell of wealth. Got you excited yet?'

'Don't be disgusting!' she hissed. 'Get away from me!'

'You can't eat this, Claire,' he went on remorselessly, pressing a wad of money against her trembling lips. 'You can't drink money and you can't cuddle up to it at night. But who cares? It gives you power—and the illusion that it can make your dreams come true——'

'Stop!' she cried, pushing his hand away. 'Stop!'

She clapped her hands to her ears and shut her eyes to block out his malevolent expression. Trader worshipped money. He had a lust for the power it could bring and the dreams he thought it could fulfil. She pressed her fingers hard against her scalp and squeezed her eyes tighter still.

Trader's hand brutally jerked one hand away and she shot him a frightened glance. 'What will you do to earn this?' he asked softly, waving the money at her. 'A thousand pounds. Is that enough to get you on your back? No? Prefer credit cards?'

'For God's sake, Trader!' she said hoarsely. 'This is getting out of hand! You're over-reacting——'

'I tend to,' he said grimly, 'when I put my faith in someone and they let me down. I don't like that. I'm used to making good judgements. To being in control and making well-thought-out decisions that others carry out. It's years since anyone made a fool of me; years since I was humiliated and made to suffer the consequences of a hasty action—and I don't like being reminded of the way it felt. Not one little bit. I went under that time. It won't happen again. This time I'm going to kick back.'

As though he felt disgusted with himself, he threw the wad of notes to the floor. Claire waited in the frozen silence for him to pick them up. After a while, when he did nothing other than scowl darkly at his wedding-ring, she realised that pride was going to prevent him.

'You can't leave that there!' she said, intending to reason with him.

He turned glittering eyes in her direction and raked her from head to foot. 'You take it,' he said coldly.

Claire hesitated. It was her money by rights. There was enough to make her mother's life easy for a while. 'And if I don't?' she asked haughtily.

'It stays there,' he sneered. 'The chauffeur is too honest to touch it and he'll move it to hoover the carpet and then he'll put it back again. I imagine that whatever doesn't blow out of the window will remain there till it rots.'

'That's wasteful!' she remonstrated.

He shrugged as if he didn't care. A thousand pounds! She knew he was watching the struggle going on inside her and mocking her indecision. But she couldn't let that much money sit there doing nothing when there was a good cause waiting! Her fingers twitched on her knee.

'Go ahead,' he taunted softly. 'Everyone else is corrupt. I know you are. Why pretend otherwise?'

Claire winced at his cynicism and began to colour up because she knew he'd misinterpret her action. 'It's not for me,' she said stiffly, her voice becoming muffled as she bent to scoop up the pile of notes. The blushes multiplied. 'It's——'

'Spare me the explanation,' he drawled in contempt. 'Just take it, stuff it in your bag and let the warm glow of possession settle over you. I'd rather you were open about your motives. At least I'd know how to treat you then.'

Flushed and flustered, she sat back again and stared at the small fortune in her hands. 'And how is that?' she mumbled miserably.

'With contempt!' he rasped. 'I should have listened to advice and realised that you weren't everything you seemed——'

'Whose advice?' she demanded indignantly.

'Never you mind!' he growled. 'But you are as amoral as your father——'

'Stop it!' she yelled mutinously.

'Why? Does your conscience prick you that when Diana died she left your father everything? The whole damn fortune?'

'Why should it?' she snapped. 'Who else would she leave it to, but the husband she loved?'

He drew back suddenly. 'Who else indeed?' he said softly.

But it was a savage softness, born of a sour hatred. Envy, too, she assumed, because apparently Trader had coveted her father's wealth for years. And so he'd copied her father's methods of getting rich. Her heart was stabbed with pain. The similarities between the two men were frightening.

Trader took her limp hand in his and fingered her engagement ring thoughtfully. And then his dark, mesmeric eyes flashed up to meet hers with a fierce intensity that made her draw back in alarm.

'Tell me, Claire, do you want me to share all my worldly goods with you, as Diana le Trebisonne shared hers?'

'Marriage *is* sharing,' she answered in a whisper, squirming under his hard, avaricious gaze.

'And if I continue to deny you your "share"?' he asked coldly.

She glared, then sharply lifted her head with its flame-coloured curls bouncing in protest, proud and determined to show Trader how little money should mean to anyone. And that she would sweep the past under the carpet and start again to build a good marriage.

'That would be immoral,' she said firmly. 'We——'

'Then I want sex from you in return,' he grated, interrupting her. 'Marriage is sharing,' he mocked.

'But we don't have a conventional marriage, do we?' Claire shot, barely keeping the misery from her voice.

'Then we make our own rules,' he murmured. 'The more you give, the more I give. How's that for a neat and tidy arrangement, you little whore?' While she gaped at him in bewilderment, he slammed back the privacy blind. 'Driver!' he ordered furiously. 'Take a right! Go down to the beach!'

'What—what are you doing?' she demanded nervously.

'Taking a detour,' he snapped. 'Worried about missing your exotic, expensive honeymoon?'

'No! Not in the least!'

'Well you bloody well ought to be! You'll be earning your keep during it, all night, every night!' he growled.

'My *keep*?'

'What you've got there in your hot little hand won't last long, will it? I'm in control of the money,' he growled. 'Not you. It's *mine*, Claire!' His eyes gleamed with triumph. 'What you want, you'll have to work for. On your back. Night after night, after night. Day after day, after day. Get the message, *darling*?'

CHAPTER SIX

CLAIRE froze in horror. Her hopes of making the marriage work were shattered into a thousand pieces. She gave a little moan and closed her eyes, concentrating on keeping down the sickness in her stomach as she sought to find something that would keep them together on vaguely civilised terms. And failed.

She'd fallen for a man who was strong and caring and honourable. A man who'd fitted into her life like a hand into a glove. They'd been like kids, making sandcastles, building dams against the sea, fishing for shrimps in the little rock pools of Ballymare. And he'd even tempted her mother into the ocean, helping her to jump the Atlantic rollers, holding her safe and secure while she squealed like a joyful child.

Claire's face screwed up in pain. She'd loved him for that! Her mother was having fun for once in her life and Trader's kindness had melted her heart. His easy smile and frequent laughter had brought sun into their lives.

It had been an act, she thought dully. 'Oh, God!' she groaned.

He grabbed her arm, his hand closing over it tightly. 'Let's get one thing straight, shall we?' he said with soft anger. 'Marriage hasn't made you an instant financial partner as far as I'm concerned. I spend it any way I like. I will not be tied down by my wife! I need freedom, understand? You don't interfere in my affairs and I don't interfere in yours.'

Her dull, tired and bewildered brain was whirling in confusion but it caught a keyword. 'Affairs? What affairs? What affairs are you intending to have while my back's turned?' she demanded shakily.

'My God!' He jerked back as if she'd hit him. 'You've accused me of almost everything apart from murder today! Isn't there one bone in your body that trusts me?' he asked bitterly.

Claire felt her eyes fill with tears. He didn't love her. He'd never loved her. Her marriage was all but over. A few blissful hours and then years of unhappiness. Worse than her mother's record.

'No,' she mumbled. 'I don't think there is!'

Trader twisted his head away as if he couldn't bear looking at her. 'Stop the car! Stop the bloody car!' he roared, clenching his fists tightly on his knees.

With the beach in sight, the bewildered chauffeur slammed on the brakes and Trader stormed out, striding down the little lane and forging across the soft sand and over the glistening flats till he'd reached the edge of the sea. Where he stood, letting the wavelets lap at his Gucci loafers.

Claire huddled in the back of the car, humiliatingly conscious of the chauffeur's rigidly unmoving head. And she remained motionless, her brain numbed with misery, watching the tide creep around his shoes and then begin to wash over the toes.

What was he doing? She stared at him, quite bewildered by his behaviour. The waves rolled in and he seemed oblivious to them.

'Er... like me to get him, Mrs Benedict?' called the chauffeur tactfully.

Pale and wan, she kept her head turned away to hide her misery. 'No,' she croaked. 'I'll go. I'm sorry... This must be difficult for you——'

''S'all right,' said the chauffeur awkwardly. 'I'm married. It's not always a bowl of cherries, married life.'

'No. You get stones too.' But they'd only been married a few hours. It should have been bells all the way for at least a year or so.

A lifetime of frugality and care of her few clothes and possessions forced her to move as the seawater began to flop quietly against his pale grey linen trousers. Ralph Lauren, she remembered wearily. He was a mass of labels. Calvin Klein underwear...

She paused in the act of heaving herself out of the car. As she stood wearily in the pretty lane awash with wild flowers and bird song with her eyes riveted by Trader's chillingly bleak back, she asked herself how Phoenix knew what underwear Trader favoured.

Fee had shopped for him, she told herself. He'd sent her out to buy his clothes. Or...

She put a hand to the car to steady herself, weak with dismay. It was obvious. The evidence had been staring her in the face all the time; he and Phoenix. Could Fee be the love of his life? Surely not! Fee had been kind and generous, a good friend.

But... Phoenix couldn't marry until she was thirty. Was that why Trader had opted to marry an heiress till Fee came into her inheritance?

Aghast at the sudden solution that had slipped into her head, she thought about the way Phoenix had looked at Trader, with that certain expression in her eyes, and Claire groaned aloud at her blindness. Fee and Trader were in love.

Subconsciously she'd known all the time, but she'd blocked it from her mind. They knew everything about each other. Phoenix had known how he liked his drinks, what his favourite music was, and she'd even whisked away his avocado at the wedding breakfast—one of his pet hates, she'd explained—replacing it with a seafood surprise which she'd prepared herself in the hotel kitchen. 'I know how you like it, darling,' she'd murmured, laughter in her voice.

And he'd grinned rakishly and replied, 'You certainly do, gorgeous.'

Claire trembled. *It* could refer to sex.

Snatches of conversation flew into her mind. 'When Trader and I were in Kenya . . . Trader *loathed* leaving Japan. I had to cancel our accommodation to get him home... We always go horseback riding together once a week, wherever we are . . .'

Judging from their easy intimacy, it was a warm, loving relationship and had been so for some time. She frowned. Was she being paranoid? The awful thing was, that she couldn't blame him if it *was* true. Phoenix had so much more to offer. Her talk was light and bubbly, full of references to things she, Claire, didn't understand: opera performances, clever novels, the state of the Bundesbank, the FT index.

And she felt awkward and lumpen and country-bumpkinish beside the glitteringly fascinating Phoenix, who'd reeled off hilarious stories at the wedding and had kept everyone amused with her wit and repartee.

Claire looked down at herself. Slim, curvy, but not as tall as Phoenix, nor so perfectly groomed to the final eyelash. Her beige suit was attractive but the hem didn't hang as well as it should because her mother had made it.

For the first time in her life, Claire railed against her poverty. And then felt ashamed. Trader ought to love her for what she was, not because she wore devastatingly flattering clothes.

Phoenix had known him all her life. What had she said? Her spine chilled.

'Of course,' Phoenix had ruminated, knocking back her third brandy the night before, 'Trader's got a ruthless streak in him that scares me sometimes. I suppose that's why he does so well in business. No heart.' She giggled, evidently a little tipsy. 'He can twist women around his little finger. I shouldn't be telling you! It's why women fall over themselves to get in his bed, of course. Women love a heartless rogue,' she added wistfully, staring into space.

'Do they?' she'd asked, her heart beating hard.

Phoenix had shrugged, but her eyes were unhappy. 'I'll say! I fell for one long ago. I only hope he'll still be around when I'm able to marry.'

Claire shivered, remembering the misery in Phoenix's voice. Blindly she began to walk down the lane. It was all slotting into position. She thought of Diana le Trebisonne's loveless marriage to Philippe and her father's passionate courtship that had made Diana defy society and marry a man who'd been her chauffeur. Trader was passionate. Trapped in a loveless marriage, he'd need someone else to give his passion a release. Phoenix.

Her steps slowed. Could he be so cruel, so calculating? To marry with the intention of being unfaithful from the start? She let out a low groan. Yes. Trader had shown the deadly combination of volcanic passion and steely determination. He'd go through the pain and suffering of a miserable few years with an unwanted wife to get what he wanted: enough money to become Phoenix's equal.

The horror of it brought her to a halt. What a farce! Her lower lip trembled. She clenched her fists, feeling her nails digging into her palms. And she wanted to drag those nails down his face, to scar him for life so no woman would ever look at him again!

'I hate him, I hate him, I hate him!' she rasped under her breath, her eyes fixed on his brooding figure. Now *her* back was against the wall. And all she felt was the need for violence. He was right, she thought bitterly. You learnt a lot about yourself when there was nowhere to go but full steam ahead, and to hell with whatever stood in your way.

'Brute!' she moaned. Why hadn't she acted on the hints that had been dropped, or heeded the warnings?

You'll have great sex, Phoenix had said—and that *must* have been first-hand knowledge! It must have cost Phoenix dear to imagine Trader in his new bride's arms, she thought bitterly. And how painful it would have been, to say goodbye...Claire groaned. Now she knew why Trader had been so long taking the phone call and why Phoenix had emerged looking dishevelled. They'd made love. At her *wedding*!

She wrung her hands and sobbed silently, defeat suddenly killing her anger. Stumbling along blindly, shaking with distress, she cried for the wreckage that was her marriage. For better, for worse! She'd got the duff end of that promise!

Her spindly heels stuck in the sand so she took them off and, after a moment's hesitation, slid her hand to her thighs and felt through her skirt for each suspender button till she'd snapped it free and could ease down her stockings with some modicum of decency.

Barefoot in the softly sifting sand, she padded silently towards Trader, wondering what on earth she intended to do. Talk. Tell him he could go to Phoenix—that he should, if they were in love. She stumbled, choking with misery and tried to hold herself together.

She didn't care about the money. Only that her father wasn't blackmailed. If he went to prison, it would literally kill her mother. It was the only promise she wanted from Trader and she'd give up any claims and walk away from him in the clothes she stood up in if he'd agree.

Knowledge of his relationship with Phoenix had swept away the strength she might have had to fight for what she wanted. You could fight *with* love, but not *against* it.

Goodbye, she said to his back. Goodbye.

'The water's ruining your trousers,' she croaked, and couldn't go on.

He looked back over his shoulder at her, withering her with a long, slow glance. 'Dammit! Is that all you care about?' he snapped.

She flinched and stuck to banalities because she daren't open the floodgates of her emotions till she felt more in control. 'It's a waste of good clothes——'

'Oh, for God's sake!' he said impatiently. 'Life isn't about grasping material goods in one greedy hand and protecting them from harm! This is life!' he said, waving a hand at the view. 'Being in love is life!'

'I know.' Her hooded eyes hid her pain. 'I only meant to persuade you——'

'I think we've gone beyond that point,' he said acidly. 'I *knew* I should never have done this! All I wanted was——'

'Yes?' she prompted, when he stopped suddenly.

'I want the woman I love,' he said quietly, his expression bleak and haunted. 'I want her to love me. I want to be with her forever.'

She gave a sharp intake of breath as the agony split her heart. It was pain on his behalf, not hers. Dear God, she loved him so much that his hurt was worse than her own! Well. She'd make it easy for him.

'And I want a separation,' she husked. 'I have conditions, though——'

He clamped brutal hands on either side of her waist, lifted her into the air and held her dangling above his grim face. 'No,' he muttered with a rasping hatred. 'However much I loathe the idea, you and I are sticking together. I've given up too much for this. I won't let you hold me back now. I'm going for all I can get.'

'Why?' she moaned, choking with distress. 'What's the point, without love?' she cried, wriggling in his grasp. 'What do you mean?'

'I mean, you slippery little cat, I don't get what I want if you leave!'

'*What*?' Claire froze and stared down at him in horror. Her father must have insisted Trader stay with her, as part of the agreement! That had never occurred to her! And she cursed her father silently for condemning her to such a torture.

Slowly Trader lowered her while she pummelled his chest, desperate for her freedom. And then he let her slip; one fast, intimate slide against his body and a sudden landing in the icy sea.

'Ohhh!' she squealed. 'My suit! My——'

A ravaging mouth had covered hers. Great iron bars of arms had dragged her forward, the impact against his rock-solid chest pushing the breath from her body. Beneath the hot, explosive kiss, Claire fought for air, came up, gasped, and gave a whimper in her throat.

And struggled with all her might, kicking, wriggling, snatching at him with her teeth, scrabbling with her hands till they were captured and twisted behind her back. Then he had her in a brutal, savage hold, his mouth forcing down on hers and she wasn't sure if she felt elation or hate, hunger or disgust because she was kissing him back and moaning into his mouth, trading kiss for kiss, hunger for hunger.

Trader found the warm, inviting cavity of her mouth and there was such a wonderful, delirious feeling in her veins that she couldn't fight any more. She sank helplessly into his embrace, flinging her arms around his neck, responding with her tongue in such a shockingly adventurous exploration of her own that she blushed even while she pressed eagerly against him because she desired nothing but contact, kisses, new sensations.

Pleasure stole over her with a merciless insistence, heating her blood, his hands moving faster and more urgently over her body. And he groaned in his throat, gasped, savaged her mouth, her jaw, her earlobe ...

'Trader!' she cried weakly. 'For pity's sake——'

'I want to possess you,' he muttered.

'You do!' someone cried, a long way away.

'Hell.'

Her hands snaked in his hair, and she moaned, drawing him harder to her mouth, punishing herself for her madness with her own fierce kisses. This was another woman. It wasn't her. She'd been sold to the Devil and he'd wrought a malevolent magic on her, tempting her with her own hidden sexuality, dredging it up from the depths of her being where she'd saved it for the man she loved.

'I hate you!' she moaned.

'That'll do,' he said roughly.

'Brute! Brute!'

'Hold me!' he urged. '*Hard*. Kiss me. *Harder*!'

Her tongue meshed with his, and because she was being tortured by the plundering invasion she tormented him back, arching her body against his and pushing her hands beneath his shirt to feel the broad flat planes of his smooth chest.

It was desperate and urgent and hopeless. It was barbaric, raw and savage, and it wasn't love. But it was a kind of wild, uncontrollable need in her to be close to him, to know what Phoenix had known before he finally left her with nothing.

Oyster-catchers screamed overhead. The madness left her for a brief moment and Claire came to her senses, remembering with embarrassment the waiting driver.

'Trader!' She jerked her head back, frantically dodging his voracious mouth...saw the heart-stopping angle of his head, the flutter of his lashes...allowed him to kiss her, oh, so gently, with such terrible sweetness that she began to cry.

And he crooned and lulled her, kissing her eyelids, his mouth and then the tip of his tongue brushing her heavy, weighted lashes. Exhaustion was claiming her. Or was it defeat? She hardly knew and certainly didn't care. *This* was what she'd wanted: a husky timbre to his voice as he murmured flattering lies, a pretence of love in his smouldering eyes.

'The driver——' she mumbled drowsily.

'Poor guy.' Trader kissed the tip of her nose. 'He'll want to get home. Come on.'

Puzzled by his human concern, she allowed him to unwrap her from his body. With a return to reality, came a deep humiliation. She hadn't meant to behave like that! Blinking in confusion, she eyed her salt-soaked skirt in horror.

'My skirt!' she wailed.

'What the hell does it matter? We'll change.' He took her hand and walked with her across the sand.

'It's my only good outfit,' she said miserably. 'Have you any idea how much this material cost?'

'I think I can guess,' he answered gravely. 'We can put on jeans. Who cares?' His fingers touched her bruised mouth in drowsy desire. 'We know what we want now——'

'No!' she said hoarsely, knowing what his eyes were telling her. 'No, Trader! I was angry——'

'You fool!' he growled. 'That wasn't anger! It was good, old-fashioned lust. The chemistry between us is explosive.' He proved it, by running his palm over the curve of her small waist and letting it steal to the womanly swell of her hip. Her loins contracted immediately and he smiled. 'A volcano,' he murmured, jerking her into his pelvis. And there, hard and urgent, she felt his need and her eyes half closed with the exquisite languor that flowed through her body.

'I despise you!' she whispered.

'Mutual. Unfortunately our bodies don't care,' he drawled and let his tongue play with the corner of her mouth.

'I don't understand that,' she croaked and when she lifted indolent lashes, her soft green eyes widened at the terrible bitterness in his face. Disgust twisted her mouth. 'Let me go!' she moaned. 'Leave me *alone*, Trader!'

She turned her head from side to side but his hand drew it back and his mouth silenced her till she was clutching blindly at him. Loving and hating him at the same time. She wanted his heart and his mind, his emotions, his body. But she knew with a sickening shame that she'd willingly settle for any one of those, without the others. Anything, anything, to have a small part of him.

That was her love, she thought, as he deepened the kiss. Unconditional, irrational, helpless.

'You can't expect to walk away,' he said softly. His mouth brushed her ear. 'We can't leave one another. You *have* to come with me, Claire. You know you want to. God knows how we're going to sort this mess out, but we need each other——'

'No!' she protested, trying to act sensibly. 'I can't live a lie!'

'Stay for the sex.' He drew her lower lip into his mouth and she abandoned herself to the sweet taste of him.

'Not for the sex,' she muttered resentfully when he released her.

'I need you,' he said softly.

Her eyes closed in anguish. He needed to get his hands on her inheritance. 'Trader,' she began jerkily, steeling herself to denying what she wanted so badly. 'This won't work and you know it. We ought to level with each other. There is no love between us. Our marriage is dead.'

'As a doornail.' He sounded casual but there was a nerve rippling the skin at the corner of his mouth.

Somehow Claire held on to her self-control. 'We'll find a way to ease ourselves out of this awful situation,' she said quietly, proud of the fact that most of those words were steady. 'Some arrangement where we can both have what we want.'

'I'm amazed at your chillingly philosophical outlook,' he drawled, the lights in his eyes almost narrowed to splinters. 'You're quite a surprise, Claire.'

'I don't believe in crying over spilt milk,' she answered grimly. 'Mother and I have had a hard life. We've learned to roll with the punches and come up to fight another round.'

He nodded slowly. 'Yes. I understand that. I understand everything you've done.'

'Fine.' Strangers. Polite, cold and light years away from the way they'd been only hours ago. Claire clenched her jaw and focused her eyes and her mind on the horizon. 'I imagine this is going to be the most civilised and the briefest marriage of convenience on record,' she said with a disguising laugh.

Trader laughed too, but without mirth. 'Can't win them all. Pity,' he mused silkily, his eyes driving a raw message of sexual need into her receptive body. 'The sex with you would have been memorable. What a waste.'

He'd abandoned his attention to seduce her! The raw jolt of disappointment hit her like a blow to the stomach. And she wondered if she had her mother's passion for bastards—or her father's insatiable hunger for sex. Or an awful mix of the two.

'What do we do now? I—I don't think I can face anyone at home,' she said, white-faced.

'Nor me.' He frowned. 'God! Think of the gossip! The sniggers, the endless sympathy, the compassion in everyone's eyes, the humiliation——!'

'Don't!' she cried in dismay.

'What do you *want* to do?' he asked curtly.

'Hide,' she said in a small voice. Curl up and cry in private.

He thought for a moment. 'No problem. We could hole up in a hotel for a while,' he suggested eventually, his eyes slanted at her.

'A hotel?' she said uncertainly. 'Where? I don't have much cash——'

'I would pay,' he drawled.

'Yes. I think you should,' she said tartly. Her head jerked up. 'We'd have separate rooms, of course! Better still, separate hotels in separate cities!'

'That goes without saying. Both of us want to be alone, I think. Somewhere in Cork for you?'

'I don't care,' she replied listlessly.

He hesitated. 'We could give ourselves a break,' he said slowly, as though an idea was making itself known. His dark eyes flickered to hers, his expression thoughtful. 'A place where no one knows us. Where we can be completely alone, act as we wish and sort ourselves out before we have to face everyone we know with our decision to separate. Somewhere our nerves and our tempers can heal. We already have accommodation. It's waiting for us.'

She frowned. 'You don't mean in the Seychelles? We wouldn't be able to catch the plane now——'

'It'll wait,' he said laconically. 'I hired it. There are no other passengers.'

'You—you *hired* it!' She gasped. 'A private jet? My God, Trader! You throw money around like— like——'

'It's paid for,' he said, his eyes dark with irritation. 'Too late to whine about the cost. We might as well take advantage of it. A holiday in Paradise will do a lot for our frayed edges.'

'I don't want to be with you,' she said stiffly.

He shrugged. 'The island's big enough for us to avoid each other. Think of it, Claire. A sun-kissed island and several hundred palm trees. Deserted beaches. A large villa with three bedrooms and several discreet servants. We can keep clear of each other till we're ready to discuss our separation calmly,' he said persuasively. 'It would be a blessed relief to be some-where relaxing. I don't know about you, but this day has been hell for me.'

'Yes. Me too,' she whispered.

He rested a hand on her shoulder and gazed deeply into her eyes. 'I know this situation is difficult at the moment,' he said huskily, 'that neither of us is in a mood to talk, but we have to discuss what we're going to do. Division of goods, that kind of thing.'

She winced. And tried to decide how sincere he was. He'd capitulated rather too quickly—unless he was being pragmatic and hoped to get some kind of financial settlement for himself.

'I hope you're not going to be difficult about money,' she muttered.

'I could waive a few demands,' he said softly, 'given some incentive to do so.'

'Like . . . what?' she asked, her tongue nervously wetting her lips.

Again that direct sexual challenge from his glittering eyes. Slowly he raised an arm and let his hand curve around her neck. 'I might let you coax me,' he murmured, his fingers setting her body on fire with the maddening caress.

'No!' she whispered, miserably incapable of moving away.

He smiled. 'A fortnight of friendly chatting, adult to adult. Swimming in the sunset, a brisk rub-down and early to bed. Nice and friendly. End it amicably. What do you think?'

'Give me a moment to think about it,' she said huskily, feeling she was being driven along a path of his choosing again.

'We might as well continue to Cork in the meantime,' he murmured, the sensuality of his mouth making her gulp. 'If you don't agree to the Seychelles idea by the time we've arrived there, we can find a motel.'

It didn't sound as attractive as an island in Paradise. As they walked back, she mulled over the fact that he didn't mean any of that rubbish about a platonic arrangement. She knew that, he knew that. He was panting softly, a feverish light in his eyes. For a brief split-second, she let her eyes flick down to his hips and confirmed what she'd been certain of anyway. He still wanted her as badly as she wanted him.

And she could have him. It would only take one word.

CHAPTER SEVEN

THE sound of Trader's laboured breathing filled the air, and it seemed to vibrate inside Claire. She gave a little shudder.

'Tempting, isn't it?' he murmured huskily.

She swallowed the lump in her throat. 'Tempting.'

They were married. They hated one another; she despised him, but she loved him too. How that was possible, she didn't know, only that it was true and that he was tearing her heart from her. Her eyes gleamed like bright emeralds. She didn't want to give him up to Phoenix. For a little while she wanted to pretend that they were husband and wife and were happy.

No; she was lying to herself. There was a tiny, forlorn hope that if they could be together, and alone, then he'd find love with her and she would have a chance—slim, but all she had—to win his heart.

She'd never been so stupid in her life before. Or so contrary. Trader swept her along like a capricious wind, turning her one way and then another. And she swayed and bent to his will because he had captured her heart and imprisoned her soul in his black, sinful eyes.

The thrill of lovemaking and its deeper promises had hit her like a thunderbolt, destroying all her years of denial. In fact it hadn't been a real denial: she'd never been tempted to distraction before. But the moment she *had* been tempted, she'd flung all caution to the wind and abandoned all sense for the chance to release the crazed wanting that was making her tremble every time he looked at her or touched her.

'Yours.' He handed her shoes and stockings to her, a hot, hungry look on his face.

Her breath caught in her throat and a little whimper sounded there. 'Thanks.'

He was waiting for her decision. 'Cork, then Heathrow.' It was a statement, seemingly without any emotional ties. But the greed of his mouth gave the lie to its flat, non-committal tone.

Still she hesitated, fighting off the curl of heat within her receptive body. This would mean two weeks of sex. Animal needs. Primitive hunger, quickly, rawly satisfied. She shouldn't even be considering this idea. Where was her dignity, her pride?

'I don't know,' she breathed.

'Yes you do,' he said brutally. 'I'll carry you over the tarmac to the car,' he said curtly. 'We'll change. We can't wear these wet clothes.'

'But——'

He swept her up in his arms and she allowed herself the brief delight that afforded her, to have his solemn face inches from hers, the faint scent of his skin wafting down to her. He placed her gently by the boot and opened it.

'Now. We'll find your jeans. This is your case,' he said jerkily. 'Where will they be?'

She bent her head and they were almost cheek to cheek as he rummaged around in her case for dry clothes. Their hands touched, their fingers locked and she gasped at the spasm of hunger that tore through her body.

'There . . . there they are,' she muttered, relieved to see the denim beneath a soft, powder-blue sweater.

'Jeans, the jumper and . . .' His head twisted. He kissed her.

Helplessly she tried not to kiss him back, though she was frantic in her need to taste him for as long as she could. All too soon he'd be out of her life. The tears began to roll down her cheeks.

'Don't,' she mumbled against his mouth.

But it became marauding, his hands gently holding her a more than willing prisoner, the cruel skill of his lips joining with the love in her heart to make her an easy victim. And it became harder and harder for her to flail at his chest.

'Heathrow,' he whispered, and, ridiculously, it sounded like the entry to Paradise, because it was husked into her mouth and accompanied by a heart-stopping caress of her lips by his and an achingly drowsy plea from his smouldering eyes.

'In jeans?' she croaked, trying for something, anything, to break the spell.

'Nothing more sensible for travelling,' he murmured. 'I'll find mine. You can change in the car.'

'I don't think——'

'I wish you wouldn't,' he said wryly. 'I'd rather you reacted and did what you wanted to, instead of what you should. Claire, let's not waste this opportunity. We can be together. How long, how short that time will be, we can't tell. But we have something unfinished between us. Don't we?' His fingers tormented the curve of her cheek, played with sun-shot strands of her hair, and then he was holding her face between his hands and kissing her stupid again.

'Lust,' she said bitterly.

His eyes glittered. 'Yes. Good, honest, old-fashioned lust. With a holiday thrown in. If nothing else, we'd get the demons out of our systems. At the moment they're driving us crazy. It would be better if we got our urges under control, wouldn't it? We won't rest till we've made love. This is our opportunity. Better than nothing, don't you think?' he coaxed.

'Oh, Trader!' she sighed in despair. And thought to herself, because it was a secret for no one else to hear, Yes, I do!

'I know. It hurts like a knifing pain. Unfulfilled sex is like that,' he said softly. 'On the island, we can talk under the stars. We can ease our physical needs. I can tell you my life story and you can tell me yours. We can become friends. Perhaps that's our destiny, Claire.'

'It sounds almost civilised,' she said wryly, wavering. 'Logic tells me that it would be such a waste not to go, but——'

'Of course,' he agreed. 'After all, the honeymoon cost thousands of pounds.'

'Did it?' She looked shocked. 'I *told* you we ought to go somewhere nearer home,' she fretted.

'It's paid for now,' he said with a faint smile. 'You'll enjoy it——'

'I'm not the sophisticated type——' she began uncertainly.

'Neither is the island. It's very unspoilt. We won't be disturbed by telephones or fax machines or a television. The wildlife is fascinating, the diving out of this world. Sun, warm seas, good food. We should go. We need to hide away, nursing our bruises and our wounds and our disappointments till we can face the world again.'

She leant against his chest and let him hug her. It was a wonderful sensation, feeling the strength of his back beneath her splayed palms. And his deep, throaty voice whispered on in her ear, gentle, persuasive, luring her to sin. Except it wasn't real sin because they were married.

Only it was a sin in her eyes because he didn't love her. Yet. Her pulses raced. Two weeks on a remote island. Maybe it would give her a chance to salvage something of her marriage.

'I—I do want somewhere to go, away from it all. I can't face Mother with the truth yet and tell her that our marriage is a sham—you're right,' she said huskily. A holiday in the sun, whispered the voice of wickedness inside her head. Her first holiday away from home. And it would be with Trader. 'I don't see any reason why not ... but——'

'Neither do I,' he murmured throatily. 'Go into the car and change. I'll join you in a moment.'

He bundled her in before she could protest and the chauffeur pretended to be waking from a deep sleep. 'Ah. I was having a little nap! Where to, sir?' the chauffeur asked innocently.

'The airport, when we've changed our clothes,' said Trader, giving her no chance to say anything. He squeezed her hand and then kissed it. 'You wouldn't turn down an adventure like this, would you?' he murmured.

Claire hung her head. She was conniving in her own fall. But she had to be with him. 'It seems sensible. We do need to talk things over without interruptions, and as the accommodation's paid for...' she said stiffly.

But her free hand reached out tentatively to stroke the tempting hollow beneath his cheekbone and, with a muttered exclamation, Trader bent his head, leant into the car and kissed her breathless.

'See you in a moment,' he said, triumph firing his eyes. And he slipped off to change while Claire sat in frozen shock, wondering what she'd agreed to.

Holding up her jeans for the driver to see, Claire muttered a croaky, 'Excuse me!' and slid down all the car shutters so that the interior was closed to prying eyes. But although she managed to shed her jacket without any trouble, her fingers were shaking so much that she couldn't undo the waistband of her skirt. So she gave up. And that was how Trader found her; curled up on the seat like a child. And in a way she wished she were, and not a woman, with a woman's needs.

'Drive on,' he ordered through the intercom and then abruptly switched it off. Even though her eyes were closed, she knew he was watching her and she wasn't surprised when he heaved a deep sigh and pulled her into his arms.

'I have to hold you,' he said in a low voice. 'I need someone right at this moment, Claire.'

'Yes. I need someone too,' she said feebly.

Nestled cosily in the crook of his arm, her bare feet drying in the warm air, she nuzzled his neck while he stroked her thigh in a slow, steady rhythm. Her breathing became shallow. Beneath her small ear, his magnified heart raced in a satisfying way.

He wanted her. And she didn't know whether she felt pleased or ashamed. Because he was betraying

Phoenix and she—she, his wife!—was the Other Woman!

A rueful smile played about her lips but it faded as rapidly as it had come. If he could betray Phoenix so blatantly, fidelity meant nothing to him. For the duration of this holiday they would have this brief fling, and at the end of it she would have sacrificed herself for two weeks of sex. With a callous brute who was intending to leave her the minute they got back home.

She wanted to blank out that thought. It was so final. And she had her hopes, irrational though they were. She had to fight for him because it was her only chance. She had to do everything she could to be as attractive, as sexy and as fascinating as Phoenix. And then hope that he'd stay with her long enough to need her love.

First she could appeal to his sensuality. Claire swallowed and plucked up all her courage.

'Kiss me!' she ordered. 'Oh, Trader! Kiss me!'

The fire was hotter now, burning inside her unchecked. Whatever her brain told her, she knew she couldn't refuse anything he asked. His hands curved around her breasts, touching them in a way that sent her senses spinning. There was nothing in her mind now, only Trader; his hands, his body, his insistent fingers and soft, wicked mouth.

'Claire!' he said thickly. 'We—we really... must...wait!'

That didn't sound very convincing! Had she tempted him so successfully? Pride stole into her intoxicated mind. She smiled and stretched luxuriously, her eyes flaming with heat and triumph when he shuddered. She wore only her camisole now, her skirt

riding high on her thighs. His eyes went to them and
something wanton prompted her to experiment. She
reached out a languorous hand and stroked her own
skin from knee upwards and then down again, her
eyes on his all the time.

'Yes,' she agreed, hungering for him. 'You're right.
We should wait.'

Trader's mouth tightened with a savage determination. Boldly he grabbed her and lifted her astride
him. She threw her head back in a delicious shudder,
half fearing, half elated by the hardness of him against
her pelvic bones.

The soft camisole was slipped from her shoulders.
Warmth flowed over her chest where his breath burned
fiercely. And then he'd lifted her breasts from the
confines of her satin bra and was kissing them as
though they were the most beautiful he'd ever seen.

I love him, she thought tenderly, holding his head
in her slender hands. I'll give anything to be loved
back. Try anything. And she caressed his hair, adoring
the heart-stopping flutter of his thick black lashes,
the deep concentration on his strong face as he tormented each nipple into a thick ruby bud. Then he
stopped.

'Please!' she gasped, before she could stop herself.

Black, glittering eyes flicked up and then his mouth
was tugging again in the erotic rhythm that had driven
her beyond all caring. I love him, she repeated, ex-
cusing herself. Why not?

'I'm going to devour every inch of you,' growled
Trader hoarsely.

Delighted with his need, she stretched up her body,
lifting her ribcage, her eyes glazed with love as he
touched her wonderingly, running his fingers lightly

over her shoulders, dipping into her collarbone and following each movement with his eyes. And his mouth. And his tongue. His teeth.

Claire shuddered in a wicked and sensual delight. He seemed almost as desperate as she was, and the power to arouse him filled her with elation. 'Wonderful,' she murmured throatily, watching her breasts peaking fiercely in demand.

'Wonderful,' he agreed. And just looked at her greedily while she quivered expectantly with a beautiful pain.

This was all right, her instincts were telling her. He was being very careful, very gentle. Did he really want to make love to her here, in the car? Was half an hour long enough? Her brow furrowed.

'Trader——'

'Hush. Relax. Stop thinking——'

'But——'

'Just be. Enjoy. I want you,' he murmured passionately.

Stealthily his fingers crawled under her skirt, pushing down the beautiful satin briefs Sue had given her. He cupped her tight buttocks with his strong hands. Her groan of need became smothered by his mouth. Without knowing, she writhed against him, felt the springing of heat against her loins and an answering urgency in hers.

She felt sensual, languid, her eyes half shut as she swayed her slender body and listened to Trader exclaiming in hot, passionate huskiness over her skin, her suppleness ...

'Oh, God!' he groaned against her lush breasts. His breath heated her flesh and she could smell their soft perfume drifting between them. Claire moaned, her

hands stealing like small thieves to the warm planes
of his chest. Superficially he felt like satin. Beneath
the surface, however, lay iron. Her delighted fingers
explored, testing the daunting muscular power beneath the skin. 'I didn't mean this to happen,' he
muttered, as bemused as she. 'Not here. I meant it to
be somewhere romantic or exotic with music and
flowers——'

She'd found his nipple. He remained still, holding
his breath, while she slowly undid his shirt buttons,
kissed the small, hard peak, then tasted it with the tip
of her tongue. And, hearing his moan of pure delight,
she copied what he had done to her and lapped it, her
body pressed hard against his in the gesture of a willing
wanton.

There was a change in him. He'd reached the point
of no return. She sensed it with the uncanny knowledge of a woman who has recently become tuned in
to her own body—and for the first time in her life she
was intensely aware of every inch of herself, knew with
blinding clarity the parts Trader had kissed...and felt
the pulsing throb of those he had yet to reach.

Her heart lurched. She would be his. No one could
take that from her. He was demanding more and more
with every kiss, his breathing ragged and laboured,
and she couldn't hold back any longer.

'I want you,' he said urgently. 'My beautiful,
darling Claire, I want you so badly!'

He was pulling off his shirt, yanking free his tie,
his eyes fevered and hypnotic. Her face was cupped
in loving hands and for a few seconds she pretended
that he cared and this wasn't lust, but love. Joy suffused her whole body because his kiss was full of re-

strained tension, as though he hardly dared to believe that she needed him too.

'Damn you!' she whispered, but she was smiling ruefully. And fumbling with her skirt again.

'Leave it,' he said roughly, jerking it up in one swift movement to her waist. 'Leave it. I can't wait. I need you. I can be gentle now. Soon I won't have the control. Now, Claire. Now!'

She swallowed and didn't trust herself to speak. But he took her wide-eyed silence and pillowy mouth for a 'yes' and slowly eased away her briefs while she did everything she could to help him as she lay across his lap. And then his hand began to steal from the sensitive arch of her bare foot to her ankle-bone, circling it with an agonising attention.

'Please, Trader!' she mumbled, at his shoulders.

He smiled faintly and caressed her calf with his warm, strong fingers. Lightly. Delicately. Her whole body was willing him to slide his hand to the emptiness that lay inside her but she knew he was going to torture her by taking his time while her love and need for him spilled from her, leaving her weak and defenceless to his every whim.

He caressed the satiny back of her knee. The firm flesh of her creamy thigh. Claire tensed. 'Say... say something nice!' she croaked, desperate to legitimise what she was doing with even his lies.

His hand stilled and when he looked into her eyes, it seemed as though he was guarding secret feelings. 'You want me to say that I love you?' he asked softly. 'No, Claire. I won't do that for you. This has nothing to do with love, has it? You've been waiting a long time to give yourself and you're not going to pretend that this is the action of someone in love. Settle for lust. Greed. Suppressed sexuality on the verge of freedom. But not love.'

'You bastard!' she moaned, trying to escape.

But he'd pinned her down and had at last touched the hot, throbbing edge of her terrible need and she froze with shock at the intense tremors that were invading her body.

'I'll tell you that you're beautiful, because that's true!' he growled, his mouth inches above hers. 'I'll say that you excite me beyond belief, that the idea of making love to a virgin is exquisitely appealing, that your skin is soft and scented and your damn green eyes are driving me insane. I'll say that I am so aroused I could take you again and again and that I intend to do that; I'll tell you how perfect your body is, slender and lush and so sensual when it moves that my eyes are dazzled. But I won't tell you that I love you. So don't damn well ask for that ultimate in surrender!' he finished savagely.

Mad with desire and churning emotions, Claire groaned and tipped back her head and a river of amber spilled over the cream leather. He kissed her throat, his fingers gently, remorselessly drawing her to a frenzy of need as he took a deep, raw breath.

And then a bell shrilled in her ear and she almost fell off his lap. 'A *phone*?' she croaked, in a bemused voice. 'Oh, God! A phone!'

'Hell!' groaned Trader. 'Hell and damnation!' It continued to ring and they stared at one another blankly, trying to find earth again. The sound kept screeching in her ear, making her wince. So Trader dazedly reached for the receiver, lifting it from the holster like an automaton. 'Mmm?' he grunted.

Claire's adrenalin-bright eyes remained fixed on his face. She saw him blinking as if to clear his head and the slick of his tongue over his lips—and then he looked away from her as if embarrassed.

Without a word, she levered herself up and grabbed her clothes. His face said it all. Something awful had happened. Numb with shame, she dressed, dragging on her jeans with trembling hands. She licked the moisture from the groove on her upper lip and heard Trader's intake of breath. Their guilty eyes meshed and looked away again.

After a while, and a few monosyllabic responses, he replaced the phone and scowled at it for a few seconds. There was no sound but the smooth drumming of the wheels. Trader continued to stare into space with the intense concentration of someone whose mind was spinning so fast he might lose his balance if he moved an eyelash.

And then he put his head in his hands. 'Oh, God!' he said softly.

The tremor in his voice shook her to the core. 'What is it, Trader? Who was that?' she croaked.

His head turned, very slowly until his dark and unreadable eyes were on hers. 'Phoenix.'

'No! *No*!' Claire fought for breath. 'Not Phoenix!' she groaned. 'Can't she leave us alone?'

'It was important business,' he muttered irritably. But his tan had been washed with a grey tinge.

Contrition, she thought hysterically. For betraying Phoenix with such enthusiasm. '*Business*?' she snapped. 'On your honeymoon?'

'I told you I was in the middle of something vital,' he said flatly.

Claire's emotions had reached breaking point. She, who'd rarely ever cried till her wedding-day, broke into loud sobs yet again. It had been a day for tears. Trader watched her in grim silence and she sat there helplessly, gazing mournfully at his tormented face. But then he'd woefully betrayed his darling Fee, hadn't he?

She felt the tension emanating from his body, the guilt he carried. And wept for him too. He seemed to be waiting for her to stop, but she couldn't. She hated herself for being so pathetic, but there was nothing she could do to halt the flow. There was only one person who could make her happy and it was obvious that *he* wasn't going to comfort her.

'I don't know what you're doing to me,' she breathed. 'But whatever it is, I don't like it. You've make me behave like a slut——'

'Don't be melodramatic, Claire! We're married!' he growled.

'In name only!' she yelled. 'There's no marriage of our hearts and souls!' she wailed, haunted by the mockery of her situation. 'How can I reconcile myself with that? I feel crumpled and dirty——'

'*No!*' he said harshly. 'We . . . wanted one another——'

'Don't make excuses for yourself. It was raw, basic sex and anyone would have been done just as well as me,' she broke in bitterly, challenging his gasp with a flash of her hard, green eyes. She was right. He needed a woman and she'd been there. 'The truth hurts, doesn't it?' she said coldly. 'Grabbing a bit of fun in the back of a car is not how I want to behave. I don't want to *be* what you want me to be——'

'A wife——'

'A *wife*?' she rasped. 'My God, Trader, you want it all ways, don't you? A woman you love, a wife to be available whenever you feel randy, money——'

'Yes! And I want *you*,' he growled.

'Only because there's no one else around and your appetite needs feeding!' she sobbed hysterically. 'You can't treat me like this! I can't cope with it, Trader. I'm torn in two——'

'And so am I, dammit! So am I. This can't go on. Claire——' He reached out a hand to her with a cruelly tender expression in his lying eyes.

'No,' she cried jerkily, cringing from him. Whatever he might pretend about their relationship, perhaps hoping to make it easier for her to bear, his emotions weren't as deeply affected as hers. She'd seen the look in his eyes and he clearly had loathed himself. And that was because he'd wanted sex with a woman who wasn't Phoenix.

But at least he *could* have the woman he wanted, whereas she, Claire, was to be denied the love of her life. She pressed a cold, trembling hand to her forehead. Incredibly, in a moment of mortifying weakness, she'd almost allowed him to use her, to push her into his own hell.

'This can't happen again,' she said stiffly.

'Now wait a minute! We agreed. We're going away,' he said roughly, his eyes glinting.

'Yes. To talk,' she said quickly, 'and for me to rest—without being mauled by you! No sex, Trader! No touching! I'm so *tired*. I need peace and quiet. And I need to be left alone. Just leave me alone!' she cried, in a strangled mixture of anger and despair.

He continued to eye her coldly while she cried on in the heavy silence. After a long time, Trader turned his head away and lifted the blind, as though he couldn't bear to look at her blotchy, miserable face any longer, and she closed her eyes because she couldn't bear his indifference. Or the thought of the terrible loneliness ahead of her.

CHAPTER EIGHT

'WE'LL be at the airport in ten minutes. Get tidied up,' Trader ordered quietly, tucking his shirt in, frowning and fumbling with the buttons.

'I don't care what I look like any more. I want to sleep,' she whispered, drained of energy.

'Then bloody well sleep,' he rasped.

He was obviously too occupied with Phoenix to pay her attention. His thoughts were only for the woman he loved. He didn't want to be reminded of his marriage—or his embarrassing lapse.

It would suit him if she disappeared into the woodwork. I don't know why I love him! she thought in despair, and lowered her thick fringe of lashes to hide the hurt and pain in her eyes. Weakly she leant against the cushioned leather, her head beginning to roll.

Her mind became jumbled. It seemed as if Trader was kissing her, stroking her brow. He was murmuring sweet nothings, his voice racked with pain and love. But her pleasure was bittersweet because his tenderness existed solely in her imagination.

Wistfully she dreamed, in a half-waking, half-sleeping state, of the day they'd first met. She'd been struck by his kindness and concern, and her heart sank because it was obvious she was a terrible judge of character. A smile stirred her pouting lips. A memorable meeting. One to cherish.

It had been a tiring day, working a double shift with her mother at the hotel because they'd had a final demand for the electricity bill and badly needed the money. The guest in the garden suite had phoned for the housekeeper and Claire remembered how weary her mother had looked, when she'd heaved her bones from the comfortable sofa in the staff sitting-room to make her way to the far end of the hotel.

Some time later she'd found out what had happened. It had been Trader in the garden suite and he'd noticed her mother's exhaustion immediately. He'd sat her down with a large brandy and talked to her for a long time before allowing her to deal with the problem.

But her mother's absence had worried Claire so much that she'd gone to the room with a porter, afraid of what might have happened.

The door to the suite had opened to reveal Trader Benedict. Her dream man. Tall, dark, dazzlingly good-looking—but not in the untrustworthy, smooth way of her father. You knew you were dealing with a rogue the minute you saw *him*. Trader had been smiling gently, his strong-boned face suffused with a gentle happiness that appealed straight to her heart, and she'd fallen in love with him there and then.

And her first words had been embarrassingly banal! 'Good evening, sir. I'm your room maid!' And despite her sudden shyness, he continued to gaze at her almost fondly, and smile as if he had a wonderful secret and was hugging it to himself. His friendly dark eyes seemed to see directly into her soul and made her feel confused. 'I—I'm sorry to trouble you, but . . . is Mrs Jardine here? The housekeeper,' she'd elaborated, her anxiety melting by the second. 'We were a little concerned because——'

And he'd said simply, 'Mrs Jardine is fine.'

Claire stirred, a small sigh in her throat. A dreamy gentleness stole over her as she conjured up the tone of his voice, the angle of his head and the husky, soft murmur.

'She's been attending to something for me,' he'd said. But he seemed to be saying something else to her with his eyes.

That was when her mother had emerged from the bathroom and come to a surprised halt and cried half guiltily, 'Claire!'

And Claire had stared in amazement. Gone was the worry that had brought deep frown lines to her mother's beloved face. Replacing the expression of fatigue and defeat was an elation she'd never seen before. It was as if the sun had come out in her mother's life! Then—and now—she wondered what Trader had done—or said. Her mother had laughed—laughed!—when she'd probed for an explanation, and said she was imagining things.

Claire knew she'd blinked at the time, and that her huge green eyes had turned to Trader's in bewilderment. She couldn't remember what she'd intended to say. His smiling expression had drawn her to him more surely than any arrogant command. Slowly, she'd felt herself becoming weak and intoxicated at the same time, her pulses quickening as though they'd been stimulated by a machine.

Her mother had suggested, somewhere in the dim distance, that she turn down the bed—apparently ignorant of what was going on in her daughter's head.

Claire snuggled deeper into the soft warmth that enclosed her in the gently swaying car. How foolish she must have sounded then! A faint frown creased her brow when she thought that it must have been then that Trader knew he could deceive her because she was totally malleable and naïve.

The frown lifted with the soft breeze from the window, as warm as a man's breath, or a gentle, soothing finger.

Idiot that she was, she'd muttered something stupid. 'Yes. I'll—I'll get the chocolates——' And she'd been strangely breathless. She knew why. Trader had stolen her heart. Love at first sight.

'I don't need chocolates on my pillow,' Trader had said softly, opening the door wider. 'Come in, do what you need to do and then I'd be glad if you'd spare a moment to answer a couple of questions about Ballymare.'

That had been it. He'd won her over with the same effortless ease that had captured her mother. So simple. Too simple. Claire realised now that he and Phoenix must have been laughing at the guileless country bumpkins they'd tricked!

Her mind wandered as she hoped the privacy and isolation of the Seychelles island would help her to get over the pain. Two weeks to recover, to come to terms with her fate, to undo her foolish, wholehearted commitment to him and to mend the holes he'd torn in her heart. Then, *then*, she told herself, struggling to make a vow, she'd make sure that justice was done and Trader didn't benefit from her father's money.

Her jaw relaxed and she must have slept, the feeling of Trader's comforting arms still cruelly real, the hand

that caressed her hair too gentle and loving. But she
didn't dare to open her eyes in case she found that
his expression was still cold and indifferent. The pain
would be too awful to bear.

At one stage she almost woke up, but the dream
was too lovely and she didn't want to be roused from
her fantasy. Someone was carrying her and she wasn't
sure if that was real or part of the pleasurable dream.
So she imagined it was Trader cradling her in his arms,
speaking softly, whispering in her ear and rocking her
like a baby.

And for a while, she could forget till he spoke to
her more insistently and she found herself sitting on
a seat in the airport, surrounded by a bewildering
hustle and bustle.

'Heathrow,' he said, in curt explanation. 'Do you
want me to organise a wheelchair?' he asked
grudgingly.

'My brain's in trouble, not my legs,' she answered
with a cold glance.

His mouth tightened but he made no reply. And
guided her gently through the airport formalities,
treating her like a fragile piece of cut glass. Or a
prickly hedgehog, she wasn't sure! Because he remained polite and wary throughout all the procedures.

He was hoping for a reconciliation, she thought
nervously, as they were driven towards a distant
hangar and a cluster of small, private jets. Every time
he touched her, she jerked away. Any weakness on
her part would be taken advantage of. He'd make love
to her—and she'd be racked with shame and self-
loathing forever.

'God!' muttered Trader. 'I'd forgotten!'

She followed his glance and stiffened. 'That's our plane? With the silver bow around the nose?' She looked at it in horror. 'Whose stupid idea was that?' she asked waspishly.

With a non-committal shrug, he said, 'It seemed a good idea at the time. Tim,' he said to the driver, 'you'd better take that off now.'

She averted her gaze. Once she and Trader would have laughed at the bow and its silliness. Now, it was just gross. 'Quite a smooth operator, aren't you?' she said bitterly.

Trader turned her around to face him so that her back was to the plane. 'Are you going to look happy and carefree, like a normal bride, or not?' he said through his teeth.

'Not.' Why should she save his face in front of the crew? she thought mutinously.

'Damn you!' he said grimly, turning to the crew waiting at the top of the steps and his voice—even the set of his body—changed with apparently effortless ease. The consummate liar. 'Hi, everyone!' he called cheerfully. He gave her a sideways look. 'If you want a trip to the Seychelles and time to recover from this foul day, show a bit of grace for the next few minutes and try to look like a joyous bride,' he grated. 'Otherwise I'm cancelling the flight.'

'I couldn't pretend to be happy! I can't turn my emotions on and off as you do!' she protested wearily.

'Turn around. Look wan and interesting. Flutter your eyelashes at me a few times and open those big green eyes of yours as if you think I'm the only man in the world for you.'

'No!' she whispered shakily, biting her soft lower lip.

He bent his head and to the crew it must have seemed that he was kissing her, his mouth hovering tantalisingly in front of hers. But his breath was loud and harsh, his black lashes mercifully hiding his angry, glittering eyes.

'You want to be carried up the steps?' he threatened softly.

'No,' she mumbled. The kiss became real. And he was taking her in his arms with a cruel gentleness, his hands stroking her back lovingly for the benefit of the crew while she kept her mouth stiff and unresponsive. In her throat, she complained, whining her loathing of his duplicity. In her heart, she had to admit that she was close to forcing his head towards her so that the kiss gave her a chance to release the fierce feelings she was experiencing.

Before she could gather her senses, he'd turned her around. Faces swam in front of her eyes. Curious, smiling, sentimental. She winced and shot Trader a quick glance from under her lashes. 'Brute,' she muttered, blushing furiously as he dragged her unwilling body forward and up the steps to an enthusiastic welcome.

'Welcome, sir! Welcome, Mrs Benedict! We're delighted to have you aboard!'

'Thank you,' she said, and managed a weak smile, a lifetime of politeness overcoming her reluctance to make anything easy for Trader.

'I'm afraid,' Trader told the crew gently, 'that Mrs Benedict is feeling unwell.' Claire felt awful when the smiles changed immediately to concern and she lowered her head quickly. 'She'd like to be alone to recover. It's been one heck of a day. I'm sure you understand.'

'Yes, Mr Benedict, of course we do! Please ring if you need anything,' said a sympathetically smiling stewardess. And she touched Claire's arm in a friendly way. 'I hope you like the cabin, Mrs Benedict,' she added shyly, showing them in.

It was smaller than she'd expected. Claire's appalled eyes took in the red heart-shaped balloons with 'I love you' painted on them in gold lettering, the blue and pink entwined ribbons and the carnival streamers that hung everywhere. Champagne waited in an ice bucket, tempting strawberries lay heaped in pretty dishes and heavy glass vases were filled with a score or so of red roses so that her head swam with their rich, velvet scent.

'It's lovely,' she said weakly, and, because the crew had put in a lot of work, she forced a smile of appreciation. Corny. But under any other circumstances she would have been charmed. 'Thank you. And the chocolates are my favourite kind,' she added with an effort, seeing the box on a side table.

'We only carried out Mr Benedict's orders,' said the stewardess, smiling back, and then she gave Trader the kind of look that worshippers normally reserved for a demigod. Claire had a sudden urge to disenchant the woman and tell her he belonged in hell.

'And you've interpreted them beautifully, Jess. Looks great,' said Trader huskily. 'We're delighted with your efforts. Claire was amused by that ridiculous bow on the plane, weren't you darling?' he said, managing to sound besotted. She lifted her eyelashes to him but said nothing, even when he squeezed her shoulders affectionately.

Jess grinned happily. 'Nothing's too much trouble for you, you know that. We've been thrilled that you've found happiness,' she said without any embarrassment. 'But I'll leave you in peace, Mrs Benedict. If there's anything you need—aspirin, cold compress, whatever—you'll find them in the bathroom. And please call on me if you feel worse.'

'Thank you,' Claire said gratefully.

'Thanks, Jess.' Trader saw her out and then they were alone. Claire edged away warily but, when he turned back, his expression was bleak and the relief hit her like a blow because she couldn't raise the energy to fight him off, she felt so bone-weary. 'About the decorations. I'll get rid of them if you like,' he said abruptly, scowling up at them.

'No. Leave them. You'd upset Jess,' she replied stony-faced. But couldn't help a small sob from escaping her trembling lips. It would have been wonderful in any other circumstances, she thought miserably.

'That's true. Better sit down somewhere. You'll need to be strapped in for the take-off,' Trader said curtly.

She nodded glumly and chose a seat by the window. Her ears were being assailed by her favourite music: Michael Crawford singing smoochy songs. The whole cabin was a ridiculous love nest! Soft lights, a sofa, piles of cushions on the floor... He'd gone overboard to romance her and it was all a sham.

'I think you forgot the blind musicians,' she said coldly.

'Don't push it!' he snarled. 'I'm not in the mood.' Angrily he flung himself into a deeply-padded seat and snapped shut the lap-belt as the stewardess knocked lightly on the cabin door. 'Come in!' he called, looking up with an instantly acquired, but rather feeble smile.

'Ready for take off, sir. And we've just had a message from Phoenix. She sends her love——' Claire stiffened and scowled at her knees, about to object, when Jess went on '—and asked me to pass on the information that Mrs Brodie Jardine has joined Mr Jack Jardine at his house in Jersey.'

'In the *manor*?' Trader barked, and then collected himself. 'Right,' he sighed. 'Fine. Thank you, Jess,' he added tersely. 'Let's get going.'

'Right away.' Jess closed the door quietly behind her.

'You might be angry, but I'm delighted for Mother,' said Claire defiantly, seeing Trader's angrily clenched fists. 'She does love my father, you know.'

'God knows why,' growled Trader.

'Some women make mistakes about men,' she snapped.

'And vice versa,' he countered coldly.

'You certainly made a mistake about me,' she said mutinously, with a toss of her fiery head. 'And I want to call her when we land and wish her happiness.' Glancing over at Trader, she wondered why he'd gone so pale. 'I know you don't approve of him, but——'

'He'll make her unhappy again,' he said tightly. 'His sole purpose in inviting your mother to the manor in Jersey is to annoy me——'

'Why do you assume that?' she cried indignantly, over the jet's revving engines. 'Why should you automatically think the worst of him?'

'The triumph of experience over hope,' grunted Trader cynically. 'I know how Jack Jardine operates.

Don't entertain any romantic ideas about your mother finding happiness at last. There's only one way she'll do that, and it involves seeing Jack for what he is: a cheating, lying womaniser who's madly in love with himself and the pleasures that money can bring. Like a twenty-year-old female on each arm and two walking behind.' He shot her a lethal look. 'Your mother has so many admirable qualities. Pity you got landed with your father's characteristics!' he said savagely.

'Me?' she gasped. 'You hypocrite! How dare you malign me like that? And why are you being so cruel to me? I've done nothing to you——'

'What?' roared Trader. And if he'd been free, and the plane hadn't been ascending at a steep angle, she knew he would have come over to haul her out of the seat and shake her, his rage was so great. 'Nothing? You've destroyed my faith in human nature. That's the worst thing you could do. God! Every time I commit myself emotionally to a woman, she turns around and bloody well bites me!' he growled. 'I seem to have a talent for spotting charlatans at a hundred paces but no ability at all to detect deceiving women who set out to touch my heart——'

'What's that got to do with me?' she asked bitterly. 'I never came near your heart——'

'I loved you!' he said savagely. 'And you hurled my love back at me——'

'No! I know for a fact that you didn't love me! Let's be adult about this. You're in love with Phoenix——'

'*Phoenix*?' he yelled in amazement. 'Are you out of your mind?'

'Not any more. You love Phoenix,' she said doggedly.

'God! She's the last person on *earth* I'd fall in love with! We'd drive each other to suicide!' he exclaimed impatiently. 'I love her as a sister, but I couldn't stomach her in an emotional relationship——'

'Please! Have some respect for my powers of observation and don't deny it,' she groaned wearily. 'We won't get anywhere if you keep up this ridiculous pretence that you married me for love——'

'Wait a minute.' There was a glimmer of light in his eyes like a brilliant star in a dark night. As if his anger was waning. 'I don't know who's been giving you these crazy ideas. Fee doesn't interest me sexually——'

'Damn you!' Claire thumped the arm rests with both hands angrily. 'I'm not blind! She's beautiful and sexy and——'

'Sure she's beautiful,' he broke in. 'So are dozens of women I've met. But none of them have ever had your purity——'

'My innocence,' she said bitterly, tipping up her chin and glaring at him aggressively, a tumble of red hair half obscuring her view. She must look a sight. Unkempt, scruffy... He was eyeing her with sympathy and her blood boiled. 'My stupid naïveté!' she went on crossly. 'The country girl, with no sophistication——'

'That too, was appealing.' And to her astonishment, he smiled, tugging her wounded heart. 'There's something very touching and exciting about courting a virgin,' he murmured softly.

Her mouth grew scornful. 'Appealed to your primeval male need to hunt defenceless creatures, did I?' she asked scathingly.

'You touched my heartstrings,' he husked.

'Oh, don't, Trader! Don't!' she croaked, feeling close to tears again.

'Damn the take-off!' he muttered in frustration. 'Listen. I've been looking for a woman like you for years,' he said softly. 'No,' he said, when she opened her mouth to protest, 'not because of your wretched dowry. You'll believe me later when I explain——'

'Explain now!' she demanded shakily.

'No. I'm sorry, Claire, I can't. The situation is too delicate for that——'

'Our marriage is collapsing, hearts are breaking and you say you can't?' she asked sullenly.

'Let's go back to Fee,' he said gently.

'Oh, let's.'

'Sweetheart, one thing at a time. You ought to know that Fee is a *grande horizontale*. I wouldn't dream of forming a relationship with her.' His mouth quirked wryly. 'I wouldn't know where she'd been.'

'What's a grand horizontal when it's at home?' Claire asked dubiously.

'A woman who makes a career out of her associations with rich men,' he answered drily.

'You're accusing her of being a . . . a . . .'

'Whore,' he said bluntly, his eyes not even flickering when she gasped at his disloyalty.

'How can you say that about her?' she asked indignantly.

'Because *not* saying it could ruin my future. And I know you're discreet. Fee *is* a bit different in that she works as well, because she's got a good brain and gets bored sitting around apartments, or pools, or hotel bedrooms, waiting for her current boyfriend to pay her attention. But men keep her, nevertheless, shower her with money, and she obliges them by draping herself on their arms and looking gorgeous. And performing like a tigress in bed, from what I hear.' He thrust out a defiant chin. 'That's locker-room gossip. I don't know anything about her sexual performance from first-hand experience, Claire.'

Straight from the shoulder. Direct, sincere. But... 'You were so close when you danced...and saying goodbye—hugging and kissing...' she faltered.

'Sure we were! She was upset. She'd been in an odd mood ever since I phoned her to say I was getting married,' he said gently.

'Because you'd been lovers!' she accused.

'No. Never,' he replied emphatically. 'Because we've been so close. See it from her point of view. The relationship between me and Fee has been very special ever since she was a child. We are both aware that marriage will make our relationship different and less intense. We've always been affectionate and I've always been the person she's turned to in time of need. I do care for her, Claire. Would you want me to feel anything less?'

'N-n-no, but...it seemed so sexual——' she began slowly.

'No sex. No love of the kind you're talking about. That's been in your imagination. Your own insecurity.' He smiled gently. 'Was that why you were so damn peculiar?'

'It seemed obvious...'

'Thanks,' he said drily.

She chewed her lip anxiously. 'I don't know what to think,' she mumbled, putting a hand to her aching forehead. 'I really don't.'

'I've loved you from the moment I first saw you,' he said quietly. 'Love at first sight. You knew that.

You saw how I reacted to you. Hold on to that, Claire. Don't let doubts take that away from us.'

'I want to believe,' she whispered.

Trader studied her for a moment or two, his dark velvety eyes warm with love. And Claire's heart contracted, every sinew in her body tensing with anticipation. 'I think I'd better tell you a little about the Fairchilds,' he said ruefully. 'It might help you to understand why they mean so much to me.'

'Yes. Please,' she said, hope making her head spin.

'Where do I start?'

'Childhood.'

'OK.' He paused, gathering his thoughts, his black brows drawing together in a deep frown. He fiddled with his lap belt before speaking as though it was difficult confronting the past. 'Briefly, it was hell. Both at home and at school. I was pretty unappealing, I think. Unlovable,' he added with a twisted and pained smile.

She frowned too. 'I can't imagine that!'

He turned dark, unreadable eyes on her. 'I was skinny, spotty, feeble and always moping around,' he said quietly.

'*You*? But...why were you unhappy?' asked Claire, astounded.

He shrugged. 'Indifferent parents. They were unhappy and wrapped up in themselves. They had no time for me. And, as I said, I wasn't the easiest child to love. Sour faces don't win affection. Ugliness inside and out is hard for other people to find attractive.'

'If what you're saying is true——'

'It's true enough.'

And yes, she knew it was. Astonishing. He'd wrought a miracle in himself. 'You've changed so much,' she mused, her soft green eyes resting on the muscular biceps and the strong, compelling face of a man filled with self-confidence. 'You must be almost unrecognisable to anyone who knew you then.'

'Yes. You're right. No one would know me,' he murmured, a bright, splintering light making his eyes seem briefly menacing. And then he was smiling at her again. 'I'll get to that in a minute. But I was full of self-pity then. It's hardly surprising I had no friends—except Charles. He, bless him, saw something in me to like or pity, I'm not sure which, and I spent most of the school holidays with him.'

'You can see he's nice,' said Claire warmly. 'I did like him. He spent ages guiding Mrs O'Leary around the dance-floor in her wheelchair. She could hardly turn it, she was laughing so much.'

'He's a brother to me,' said Trader with great affection in his voice. 'The Fairchilds became substitute parents for me—even before mine died.'

'How was that?' she asked. 'Didn't your parents mind?'

He shook his head, his expression suddenly brooding. 'There was a violent row at home...' He stopped abruptly and scowled.

'If it's difficult for you to talk about it——' began Claire sympathetically.

'No. I want to. Some of it, anyway. Enough to help you to understand the debt I owe the Fairchilds.' He took a deep breath. 'I went to live with them permanently when I was fifteen.'

'How awful. You must have felt very lonely. People have always been loving towards me.'

'Except your father,' he pointed out.

She was quiet for a moment, remembering his visits and the upheaval they'd caused. 'He's improving with age,' she said generously. 'But apart from him, I don't know what real alienation is like.' She swallowed, aware that she was learning what an unhappy heart felt like. 'Fee would have been a little girl when you went to live with her family. Five,' Claire ventured, searching his face for clues to his inner feelings.

Trader smiled in reminiscence. 'A lovely little scrap, even then. But treated like the baby by everyone. Five brothers can be rather daunting to a little girl. She was petted and indulged but she was very frustrated being the youngest because they'd never let her do anything on her own.'

'Only you saw that,' Claire said shrewdly, loving him for his perception.

'I was the only one who talked to her as if she was a person and not some cute doll,' he agreed. 'So she trailed after me like a shadow.'

It had been a lifetime's love, then, she thought. Even when he felt ugly and unloved. Of course he must love someone like that. But what kind of love was it?

'Did the stable family life change the way you looked?' she asked curiously, wishing she knew everything about him, as Phoenix did. Every like and dislike, every incident, happiness, success.

'In a way. The Fairchilds encouraged me to work out, to build up my muscles and my stamina,' he replied. 'I slowly grew more confident, better able to cope with life. And in turn I watched Fee through her first romances, protected her from rogues, and provided a shoulder or an ear, whichever she needed.'

'During which time, you fell in love with her and proposed to her,' whispered Claire unhappily.

Trader looked a little sheepish. 'I did propose to her. Twelve years ago. And we laugh about it now,' he admitted. 'I wasn't thinking straight at the time. I'd been left at the altar by someone I thought I'd loved——'

'The heiress. Christabel,' she muttered.

'Yes! How the hell did you know?'

'Phoenix told me.'

'Fee was marvellous,' he said warmly, 'handling all the arrangements, keeping me calm, returning presents—she was so kind, so caring, that I proposed to her in a fit of gratitude.'

'And Fee turned you down because you weren't a millionaire!' Claire said wryly.

'Thank God!' He chuckled. 'I'm glad she had the sense not to take advantage of me when I was feeling sore about being jilted. It was only my pride that hurt, to be honest. Fortunately Fee's always had her head screwed on where money's concerned. It comes before her heart. She was used to an expensive lifestyle by then, funded by rich boyfriends, and she knew I could never keep her as she expected——'

'But...if you loved one another——' Claire said hesitantly.

'We didn't. That's obvious, isn't it?' He grinned. 'Or she would have said yes and I wouldn't have chosen to forget love and claw my way to the top instead. But I do love you, Claire, and the seat-belt sign has gone out and I'm coming over to prove it.'

Hastily she unclipped her belt and stood up. 'Don't rush me,' she said cautiously. 'I daren't risk...I'm not sure——'

'No.' He paused, the blackness of his eyes softened with tenderness. 'Of course you're wary. But I'll tell you that I love you every minute of the day and night if it'll make any difference. You can see that's true if you look at me, can't you?' he urged softly.

'How can I trust you? Or my own feelings?' she said huskily.

'I hope in time you will, because I'm going to keep proving it to you. But I'll leave you alone physically till you want to reach out for me. When you do, I'll be there. And I'll stay by you for the rest of our lives. You're that important to me.'

Her breath shuddered in. He reached out for a balloon, detached it, and handed it to her. 'Read the message. *I love you.* Do you think I'd risk making a fool of myself in the crew's eyes with these sentimental touches if I didn't really care? I don't give a toss what they think. I only wanted to please and delight you, to touch your heart and make you feel warmed by my love,' he said passionately.

'But——'

'Just look around,' he said gently. 'I put a lot of love into this romantic nest! Sentimental fool that I am ... I got a girl from Bantry to embroider forget-me-nots on the cushions. The symbol for true love, you see. And I know you're fond of simple, wild flowers so there are bowls of them in the bedroom back there, which I hope are perfuming——'

'Bedroom?' She flung an anxious glance at the door he'd indicated.

'For you to rest in, if you're tired on the journey,' he said drily. 'I wasn't sure if you'd want to join the mile-high club and I don't care any more. Only that you believe me. I love you.'

'Oh.' She went pink and sought hastily to divert his mind. 'Forget-me-nots. And wild flowers. No love-lies-bleeding, then?' she asked with a wry smile.

'I hope not.' A shadow passed across his eyes. 'I don't want to lose you, Claire!' he said with a wrenching, husky passion. 'I'll do anything not to lose you!'

She let out a huge sigh of relief. She believed him. Her instincts had been right. Her eyes glistened with tears of joy. 'If that's true, then you might find me something to eat before I tackle the chocolates!' she suggested happily.

He groaned in relief. 'In a moment! Come here,' he said hoarsely. 'Let me hold you.'

'Oh, Trader!' she croaked, stumbling into his arms and lifting a radiant face to his. 'Oh . . .'

And her words were lost in his kiss. He loves me, she thought, delirious with joy. After all my doubts and fears, he loves me!

CHAPTER NINE

IT WAS their last day on their island paradise. Claire shifted sun-flecked shoulders and dropped a languorous hand in the warm turquoise ocean, rocking the big hammock slightly as she let the silky water slip through her fingers.

'We go home tomorrow,' she sighed.

'Uh.'

She grinned at Trader's lazy grunt. Tanned a gorgeous deep gold, he was lying beside her, a straw hat covering his face and she was cosily nestled up in the crook of his arm. He looked as relaxed as she felt— and as content.

'I'll remember this island as long as I live,' she said complacently.

'Uh.'

Carefully, slowly, a mischievous smile on her face, she lifted both hands up to the trunk of the palm tree that supported the hammock that had been their favourite idling place during the last two weeks. The coconut palm stretched in a loving arc across the white coral beach and extended over the crystal-clear lagoon that lay behind the shelter of the coral reef. A glorious spot.

Trader had been snorkelling in the turquoise water and had come back pleasantly exhausted. But she was ready for some action. Suddenly, she heaved herself up and, swinging a long, tanned leg, she aimed a deft kick at the hammock below.

'Ohhhohhhhh....!' Trader's hot brown body fell into the ocean with a loud splash, drowning his yell of protest.

'Help!' she giggled, as he surfaced in a cascade of water, shook his streaming black hair from his eyes and looked around for the culprit. 'Help! Save me, someone!'

Barefoot and squealing for deliverance, she scrambled down from the tree and began to run over the fine, powdery sand of the deserted beach, weaving in and out of the clacking palms and causing havoc amongst the placid ground doves.

'Gotcha!'

'Oh, help again!' she cried breathlessly, as he turned her around in triumph.

'Gotcha...' he murmured. And treated her to a salty kiss. 'Penalty,' he said softly. 'You mustn't move. You mustn't do anything. Just stand there, no matter what I do.'

'Yes, Trader,' she said meekly. But her grin told him how much she was enjoying his loving kisses and he laughed affectionately at her willing captivity. They hadn't made love. Yet. But, enclosed in his arms, she knew it wouldn't be long now. And she stretched her body languorously along his, delighting in his responsive shudder.

'You are so different,' he mused, kissing her naked shoulder.

'Browner? Warmer?' she suggested saucily.

'More confident.' His eyes met hers, full of love, so dark and steady and gentle that her breath caught in her throat. 'Why is that, do you think?'

'You've given me space,' she said quietly. 'You haven't rushed me—and I'm grateful for that. You've been tender and loving and you've left me to walk and think and respected my privacy whenever I've needed it. You've waited for me to sort myself out, when you must have known you could have seduced me.'

'You're worth waiting for,' he said huskily.

'Even on your honeymoon?' she marvelled, enjoying the sensation of the rich brown satiny skin of his broad back beneath her wandering fingers. A small knot of pleasure settled in her stomach. He was beautiful. And she wasn't afraid of giving herself any more. She knew her carefully acquired tan—and her happiness—had given her own skin a glow it had never had before and she looked almost beautiful herself.

'I hear honeymoons are over-rated when they're an excuse for a sex romp and nothing else.' Trader smiled. 'We needed to forge a bond between us again, after our doubts and misunderstandings.'

'I think we've done that,' she said softly.

His hand shook for a moment as it stroked the curve of her neck and she felt his breath quicken on her forehead. 'I've always wanted you to meet me on equal terms. And for you to know that you mean more to me than my own life.' His mouth was close to her ear, nuzzling her throat.

'I do know that now,' she said, her lips curving into an irrepressibly happy smile.

Which he kissed, all along its sensitive curves, before he said, 'You're not worried about Fee any more?'

'No. I trust you,' she said firmly. 'And I'm very content just to be with you. I feel you're my friend. I've been able to confide in you and tell you about everything. I hope you'll feel more able to talk about your past soon. I know there's something troubling you and I want to share everything with you,' she said earnestly. 'We don't need a bank account full of money. Only enough to live on, and each other. You don't have to take me on expensive holidays and give me expensive presents. I'm happy with you.'

'But——'

'Trader!' Claire gently drew back a little. 'Walk with me to the house. I want to ask you an enormous favour.'

'You can have anything I can grant,' he said, taking her hand in his.

They ducked beneath the feathery causarina trees and began to walk along the jungle path. She'd fallen in love with the small, jewel-like Palm Island, set in its tropical sea. Beyond the coral reef, great ocean rollers roared and hissed and foamed and Claire felt safe from everything with Trader beside her; the world beyond a dangerous place, made secure by his presence.

'I love you so much,' she said huskily.

He paused to pick vanilla orchids and tuck them reverently in her hair. 'And I love you, Claire. Because your hair is the colour of the sun, your eyes are as green as the sea and your skin as soft as these petals. Because you are gentle and good and care nothing for the material side of life,' he went on passionately. 'And we could be happy together in a tiny cottage if necessary——'

'Yes,' she interrupted eagerly. 'That's what I wanted to say! About the dowry——'

Trader frowned. 'Yes?' he asked cautiously.

Claire smiled and touched his suddenly humourless mouth, coaxing it to smile back with her fingers.

'Don't keep it,' she said simply. 'Give it back to my father——'

'No.'

It was a gentle refusal. But a refusal, nevertheless. Yet he loved her, so she kept her head and persisted quietly. 'I want us to owe nothing to him,' she explained. 'I'd like us to give it back and then we're not beholden to him——'

'I don't have any of it left,' he said in amusement.

'Trader!' Shocked, Claire spun around to face him head on, remembering that Phoenix had said he was doing something 'dodgy' with the money. 'You can't have gambled it away!'

'No,' he answered equably. 'I gave it to your mother. And if you don't close your mouth, sweetheart, you'll get some exotic insect flying in.' He chuckled. 'You look stunned. Don't you think it was a good move?'

'Yes! *Yes*! But...why...?' Bewildered, she scanned his laughing face and flung her arms around him, burying her head in his neck. 'Oh, Trader!' she cried, her voice muffled and choking. 'You darling! You absolute, wonderful darling!'

Trader prised her away so that he could look at her. And kiss her. 'She needed it more than we did,' he whispered. 'Now since we're talking about money——'

'Don't worry,' she assured him, standing on tiptoe to kiss his nose. 'You've got your bank job and I'll work really hard. We'll manage. I'm good at budgeting. I can scrub for England, if necessary! I'll take two jobs. I've done that before. You know I can cook economically and——'

'Claire,' he said faintly, tipping her chin up. 'Don't be daft. You know I have a good deal of money! Fee told you, surely——'

'Fee? No! I don't understand! She hinted you were rather hard up because you liked expensive things. And that you envied my father's wealth——'

'I think you misunderstood,' Trader said gently. 'Fee knows perfectly well I'm...rich.' He sighed when Claire's eyes rounded in astonishment. 'You did know, didn't you?' he said, bemused. 'You must be aware that I worried for some time about your motives for marrying me.'

'*My* motives?!' she said in astonishment.

'You kept saying you'd do anything to protect your mother. I thought that was part of my attraction——'

'You're attraction enough on your own,' she said with a wry grin.

'You can't separate me from my money, though,' he said reasonably. 'Most women dream of marrying a millionaire. I know it makes me more attractive than if——'

'Million...' She choked on the word. It wasn't possible. She couldn't have married a mill... 'No,' she breathed in panic. 'No!'

He studied her silently. 'You really didn't know, did you?'

'No!' she croaked.

'You...don't look too pleased!'

'I—I'm not! Trader, I—I can't be a millionaire's wife!' she wailed. 'I don't know how to mix with people——'

'You already have,' he pointed out calmly.

'No!' she cried, appalled, thinking of his wealthy guests. And now she understood why he'd been sounding her out about the clothes he'd worn. Expensive. The clothes of a wealthy man. 'Trader, say you're joking!' The panic rose in her voice. 'I couldn't be the wife of a millionaire! All those parties and posh dances...jet-setting, smart people saying smart things, going to the opera and having "in" jokes, your friends privately criticising my accent...I can't!' she said plaintively. 'You've got to be kidding me! Say you are!'

'Sorry. I can't. How else do you think I could afford the private jet, my own crew, my own... Hey! You look ready to faint on me! Come back to the house,' he said with a sympathetic grin. 'I think you're going to need a drink to revive you. Or five.'

'It can't be true,' she breathed.

'Yes, it can. Do you realise what this means, Claire?' he said, hugging her. 'I know you love me for myself. Not my money.'

A dove pattered amiably over her feet and she looked down blankly for a moment. The dove ruffled its marbled feathers and pecked hopefully at a thread from Trader's simple cropped cotton trousers, already drying in the fierce heat. The trousers weren't at all expensive.

He often wore ordinary things. He behaved like an ordinary man—a special man, that was, but with a naturally warm and friendly manner that put other people at ease. Not like a man who could buy Ballymare, lock, stock and barrel!

'But of course I never loved you for your money!' she cried in bewilderment. 'How could I? Apart from flinging whatever you earned on a small wardrobe of labels, you didn't have much cash as far as I could see! You stayed in a two-star hotel and we didn't do anything lavish. I don't understand any of this!' she complained.

'You will in a moment,' he soothed. 'And I'm falling deeper and deeper in love with you every second my heart slams at my ribs!' He laughed, hugged her again and guided the numb Claire past the banyan trees, the papaya and tumbling jasmine.

'But why...?' She stumbled and steadied herself by placing a hand against his chest. It felt good there so it stayed, idly, absently revelling in the strength of his body. 'There are so many whys, I don't know where to start!' she said ruefully.

'We'll sit down on the deck of the plantation house and I'll explain,' he told her in amusement.

And when they were settled beneath the bougain-villaea, with glasses of frosted pineapple and a dash of some fierce local concoction in their hands, Trader heaved a contented sigh, cuddled her to him on the huge rattan seat and stretched out his long legs luxuriously.

'I did start with nothing when I was a young man,' he said quietly. 'And I had fierce dreams of being a tycoon. I worked as if I had a fever, as if I had a short time to live. I wanted to prove something, Claire.'

'To your parents?' she asked with a gentle smile.

His mouth thinned and he didn't answer but she forgave him. It must be so painful being rejected, and he'd had a lot to prove to himself, let alone anyone else.

'I do work in a bank,' he went on eventually. 'But it's for Fairchilds', and I'm a partner now, running the Boston branch. A merchant banker. I said that I took risks with money and that's true—it's my job. I decide which individual or which company to finance, and which ones to reject for loans. I judge who has potential and who will fail, and over the years I've made my adoptive father a spectacularly wealthy man.'

'I see! I'm glad you don't gamble,' she said in relief. 'And repaying the Fairchilds must have given you a great deal of pleasure,' she mused. 'But...the heiress... Did she jilt you before you were seriously rich?'

'No. We were as wealthy as each other.'

Claire raised a golden eyebrow. Fee had got the wrong end of the stick. 'Then...why did she leave you?'

'I don't know. I really don't know what happened,' he said with a bemused shrug. 'She disappeared from sight. I heard nothing from her till she rang during our reception,' he admitted. 'And threatened to cause trouble. She'd got some crazy idea that I had found myself an heiress of unbelievable wealth and was intending to fleece her!'

'You loved her?' asked Claire cautiously, remembering what Phoenix had said.

'No. I was fond of her. Now I know what real love is, I realise that what I felt for her wasn't as profound as I imagined. Oh, she adored me and we were happy enough. Both of us at that time were scared of being targeted by a fortune-hunter. We'd been chased by plenty of those,' he said wryly. 'It felt safer to marry someone in one's financial league. You get to be very wary after a while.'

'That's why you kept quiet about your money when you met me.' Claire sipped her drink thoughtfully, her mind whirling with the implications of being married to a rich man. And she trembled a little, fearing how it would blight their lives.

'It was more than that. I'd come to Ireland for a simple holiday. I wanted to find something I'd been lacking. In the endless quest for more and more millions, I'd lost an essential part of life,' he said quietly.

She looked quickly at him. His face was dark and brooding and she felt a faint disappointment that he was still holding something back.

'I'd had no time to pause and take stock of my life,' he continued. 'I suppose you could say that in Ireland I found everything I was missing: the quality and pace of life that I yearned for, the good, old-fashioned delights like talking to friendly strangers, walking along a beach and fishing in the rain with a friend. You.' He leant over and kissed her slowly before drawing back a little to gaze solemnly at her upturned face. 'There isn't a value that can be put on friendship. Or the warm glow that comes from being in love and planning a family life. That's what I want, Claire,' he said with quiet passion, gripping her shoulder tightly. 'I know that now, with a conviction I've never felt before.'

'Father said I was part of a package——' she began cautiously.

He grimaced. 'It's a rather callous way of putting it. I wanted you——'

'Then why threaten me?' she wailed in exasperation. 'You said to me that you wouldn't let me go, that you'd get nothing if I left——'

'That's true!' he cried fervently. 'I'd have nothing I wanted: love, tenderness, mutual adoration and friendship, peace, tranquillity——'

'Oh, Trader!' she breathed shakily, appalled at how she'd misinterpreted his words. 'Was that what you meant?'

'Of course—and your father could see that. He was all set to tell you that I was worth a fortune. I had to threaten him with dire consequences if he told a living soul.' He grinned. 'He would never have understood how much I loved you. So I worked out an approach he'd understand. I demanded an exchange of money and shares for my silence about his tax evasion——'

'You sly devil!' she said wryly. 'That *was* something he'd understand—total greed! I can see that Father would fall for that kind of dirty trick!'

Trader gave a strangely bitter smile. 'I wanted that money because I'd talked to your mother and discovered the difficult situation she was in, financially. I recognised her name, you see, having known your father in business for some time.'

'That was the secret between you two!' cried Claire.

'Our...yes.' Trader seemed disconcerted for a moment and then recovered himself. 'Well, it seemed very unfair that your father was keeping all his money to himself. I managed to persuade your mother that she had a right to the money——'

'Nobody else has achieved that,' Claire said slowly.

'I have a silver tongue,' he grinned. 'She has her own reasons for accepting. It makes her more his equal, you see. It gives her some independence. I'm hoping it'll mean she looks on herself in a different way.'

'How wise you are!' she sighed. 'You understand Mother, don't you?'

'I'm not sure. Let's hope all goes well for her,' he replied huskily. 'And for us. It's nearly all over, Claire. I have one more thing to achieve and then I can say goodbye to the rat-race and start living a real life——'

'Doing what?' she asked uncertainly.

'Anything. I feel I can do anything,' he grinned. 'With you. I hope to God it'll be with you.'

'Of course!' she said emotionally. 'I could no more leave you than I could live without my heart. But you could have told me all this earlier——'

'I felt like an intruder in Paradise,' he explained with a sigh. 'I didn't want that Paradise to be destroyed by talking about my money and my plans till we'd got to know one another really well. I nearly lost you because I believed that you knew I was rich and for a while I feared that you were as grasping as your father.'

Claire frowned at the scarlet Red Cardinals, sitting in the big banyan tree like exotic blooms. She thought of her mother's happiness, so precariously in her father's hands. 'My father has yet to get off the money-go-round,' she commented sadly.

'I think it's ground to a halt as far as he's concerned,' said Trader tightly.

Her head jerked around at the hard, clipped tone. 'Because you took so much from him? Have you ruined him because you decided to—to blackmail him?' she asked unhappily.

'He ruined himself.' Curt and condemning, Trader leaned forwards and picked up his glass, flicking out the red hibiscus with a quick gesture and scowling at the drink as if it were her father's face. 'He was one of the loan propositions I knew would fail. Your father came to Fairchilds' for venture capital. I loaned it to him, knowing that he'd over-reach himself.'

Claire sat up, her back stiff. 'When all's said and done, he is my father,' she said reproachfully. 'Why encourage him to expand beyond his ability to cope?'

'An old grudge,' muttered Trader.

'Then I think I have a right to know what that is,' she said firmly.

Trader emptied the glass and banged it down on the table. He gazed ahead with sightless eyes, his profile like carved marble. And then he drew in a long, painful breath. 'He destroyed my mother,' he said hoarsely.

'Oh, Trader!' Upset by his raw emotion, she curled up against him and gave him a loving, sympathetic hug, staying silent for a long time. 'I'm so sorry,' she whispered eventually, when she felt his tense body ease a little and he returned the pressure of her arms. 'I'm afraid he's always played the field. I suppose he came between your parents and caused all your misery.'

'Yes.'

'I'm sorry, darling. I really am.' She hesitated. Then plunged in. They were being honest with one another and they had to talk things out. 'You hate him, I know. And I think you're planning something unpleasant. Stop your revenge against him,' she pleaded. 'For my sake, for my mother's sake, too.'

'You support him, after everything he did to you and your mother?' he muttered.

'He's my father,' she said simply. 'I suppose I've always wanted his approval because I never had it—

he rejected me as surely as he rejected Mother.' Claire sighed. 'I was so scared, when he came to see us.'

'Did he visit much?' asked Trader gently.

'Once when I was four and then when I was a teenager. Mother went into a flat spin both times!' she said ruefully. 'Scrubbing and cleaning, trying on clothes, fussing with hairstyles for both of us ... And I was very, very good. I remember he kissed me and joggled me on his knees and then the sweets he'd given me did something terrible to my upset nerves and I was sick all over his white trousers!'

Trader grinned sympathetically. 'Was he mad?'

'Furious. He pushed me off his lap and I fell to the floor. But the worst thing was that I knew I'd spoiled my mother's happy day. Father had a way of making us both feel inferior. You've changed that.' And she smiled appealingly up at him. 'You and I are happy. We have more than most people. We can be generous to him, can't we? You don't have to harass him any longer.'

'I'll give you this promise,' Trader murmured against her hair. 'If he stays with your mother and treats her well, I won't call in the loans we've made to him and I won't expose him to the tax authorities. To repay even just the interest on the loans, he'll have to work hard because his shares are dropping and a word from us, one of the most respected merchant bankers in London, could suspend trading. But for you, I'll hold my fire. OK?'

Yes,' she said gratefully. 'Thank you, Trader. Thank you.'

He gave a contented sigh and kissed her forehead lightly. 'They're fishing for our supper out there,' he said, staring out at the little boat in the dazzlingly bright lagoon. 'Red snapper, bonito, caron.' His voice grew huskier. 'I wonder if we should go in and change for dinner?'

'But it's...it's almost three hours till...' Claire gave a gentle shudder as Trader's warm mouth drifted over her throat. And she understood what he was suggesting. A tremor ran through her. 'Yes,' she whispered, her eyes closing as she indolently wrapped her body around his. 'Three hours. I imagine we'll need that long.'

He'd swept her up in his arms before she could say any more and he was striding through the palm-screen door and over the beautiful teak floor to the master bedroom of the old plantation house. A bedroom which they'd never occupied together.

'Don't be afraid,' he said softly.

'I'm not,' she breathed. 'Because I love you.'

And she abandoned herself to the gentleness of his touch, exploring his magnificent body till her own shy passions had reached a fever pitch to equal his. Her heart and her soul belonged to him at last. His heart and his soul were hers too. However intense the physical pleasure was, it could never match the profound emotions which were aroused and sated within her.

Afterwards, they lay quietly on the Napoleonic four-poster bed, the ethereal white drapes drifting with the slight breeze, neither of them capable of speech. But speech was unnecessary and she knew that they would be happy for ever.

Outside she could hear the sound of the fishermen coming back and talking to Marie, the woman who came in to cook wonderful Creole food for them every evening. Drowsy and content, she entwined her hands with Trader's.

'Our last night,' she mused.

'We can come back. The island is mine. Whenever we want to indulge ourselves or your mother, we can come here and play Robinson Crusoe and Girl Friday again,' he murmured sleepily.

'An island!' she groaned. 'Are you constantly going to throw surprises at me?' she asked with a rueful smile.

'Not many more.'

She shivered. There was something cold in his tone. On the point of asking him to explain, she felt him drawing away. He was on his feet and heading for the shower, a worrying stiffness to his deeply tanned back.

'Trader——' she began.

He turned, his eyes black and inscrutable. 'We ought to dress for dinner,' he said flatly. 'I've asked Marie to set it on the beach. Since it's our last night, I thought we'd eat al fresco, under the stars.'

His eyes challenged hers, warning her not to delve into his secrets. And she didn't want to spoil the perfection of the day. Perhaps on the plane to Boston, she thought. There should be no secrets between them. Then her face fell when she remembered Phoenix's romantic dinner.

'Something wrong?' he asked watchfully.

'Memories of a remark.' She lifted her liquid eyes to his. 'A dinner. Smart, elegant, with crystal glasses and a mahogany table——'

'Oh, the meal with Fee!' He gave a short laugh. 'She prepared that for me once as a joke. I fell about laughing and couldn't sit down. The cheese soufflé sank and she flung it out of the window in pique!'

Claire smiled wryly. 'Can we have candles?' she asked lightly, deciding it would be wiser not to pursue that story any further.

'Candles,' he said, and smiled back in evident relief. 'The blindfold musicians could be trickier.'

They made love after the romantic meal beneath the black velvet night; languidly, exquisitely, till Claire was tormented beyond belief. And during the flight to Boston they began to explore one another again, hardly able to leave each other alone. Now the floodgates of her sexuality had been breached, Claire marvelled how their physical knowledge of each other could enhance their love. Lying beside Trader, stroking his sheltering arm, she felt more a part of him than ever; bound to him more completely than she could have thought possible.

He stirred reluctantly. 'I think I'd better make contact with our pilot. Check our flight plan.'

'Don't go,' she murmured lazily.

'Won't be long.'

He dropped a kiss on her forehead and slipped away. She slept and when he came back he woke her roughly, stripping off his clothes with a fervour as though he could hardly wait to possess her again.

She lay panting after his frenzied assault, dazed by his emotional hunger, the scalding kisses still burning on her body. 'Trader,' she husked weakly. 'I feel very ravished!'

'Did I hurt you, darling?' he asked with tender concern. 'I needed you so *badly*!'

'I noticed!' she grinned, and wriggled her smooth, golden body appreciatively. But he remained tense and strung up. Puzzled, she rolled on top of him and gazed into his black, glittering eyes. 'Are you all right?' she asked. 'You seem ... like a sprinter, waiting on the blocks!'

'I've never felt better in my life,' he cried, treating her to a dazzling grin. 'But I'd better tell you that we're making a detour. To the Channel Islands. I need to do something in Jersey before we go on to Boston. OK?'

'Business? Something's made you sparkle! Something special has turned you on——' she teased.

'Business,' he said with a satisfied sigh. 'It won't take long. And then I'm all yours again.'

Content that he was happy, she snuggled up to him.

At Jersey airport, she strolled along with a blissful smile on her face, almost in a world of her own. Then she felt Trader's hand detaching her arm and he'd left her, striding over—then running, his whole body filled with an inexplicable excitement as he raced towards...

Phoenix.

CHAPTER TEN

CLAIRE stood stock still in shock. It wasn't the fact that Fee was there—it was the intense joy on Trader's face. And she remembered his exuberant behaviour after visiting the pilot and, presumably arranging the detour. He'd known he was going to see Fee and that had fired his passions to furnace-heat.

Worse. When she reluctantly dragged herself within earshot, she heard Fee saying, 'Tell her! You've got to tell her!'

'No!' growled Trader emphatically. 'I can't——'

'Tell me what?' She knew her face had gone pale beneath the tan, she could see that by Trader's expression.

Trader cleared his throat. 'Darling——'

She drew back from his conciliatory gesture. 'Tell me what?'

'Hell. Not here——'

'Yes, here!' she demanded, her heart so loud in her ears that she could hardly hear her own words. 'If there's trouble, if I need to fly home, at least——'

'No, darling. Of course you don't need to fly home!' said Trader fondly. 'You know there's nothing between Fee and me——'

'Oh, God!' groaned Phoenix, raising her eyes to the ceiling.

'I'll explain on the way,' he promised persuasively. 'Let me just make a couple of calls and we'll be off.

I'll walk with you both to the car so I know where it's parked.'

They discussed the weather. Then some story that Phoenix had read that morning in the paper about a Jersey banker who'd had a mistress for sixteen years, to the complete surprise of his wife and five children. Her heart thudded violently. Wives could be easily fooled!

They reached the car and the two women got into the back and Trader had gone before she could demur. To her dismay, his body still held that air of anticipatory elation which had chilled her heart.

'He's so thrilled to see me,' sighed Phoenix huskily, devouring Trader with her eyes. She gave a satisfied stretch of her shapely body and smoothed the skirt of her elegant cream suit. 'We've missed each other so much!'

'Yes. You've been old friends for so long——' began Claire defensively.

'Friends? It's been more than that. You have to be told. It's only kind.' Phoenix smiled warmly at the stony-faced Claire. 'You must have guessed. All the time he's been making love to you, he's been thinking of me. You've been an object to release his frustration. He's in love with me. We've loved each other for years.'

'I don't think so,' said Claire shakily. Her hand touched Fee's arm in gentle sympathy. 'I understand how you feel about him——'

'No!' Phoenix cried sharply. 'You don't! We're in love! God, you're a fool! How long will it take you to realise he's been spinning you a line——?'

'How long will it take you to realise that we've just spent an idyllic——'

'You sucker!' snapped Phoenix, shouting over Claire's rising voice. 'He does that every now and then, to bring me to heel. It's the way he behaves. He's a bastard, really. He likes a change. But he always returns to me——'

'I refuse to listen to you!' yelled Claire. 'I *know* he loves me——'

Phoenix grabbed Claire's wrist and twisted it painfully. 'He hasn't told you anything, has he?' she sneered. 'I know his body better than you do! I'm an expert in bed. Which of us do you think a sophisticated man like him would prefer? Little Miss Simple, with a vague knowledge of the missionary position, or a real woman, like me, who knows a million ways to drive a man to distraction?'

'You're evil!' whispered Claire in horror.

'That's why Trader and I suit one another!' crowed Phoenix. 'And I know why he married you! It wasn't for love. He had a better reason.'

'So tell me,' said Claire coldly.

'Revenge!'

Claire stared at Phoenix blankly. 'Ridiculous! I haven't hurt him!' she scoffed.

'No. But your father has,' said Fee with a smug expression. 'You poor sap! No wonder Trader said he couldn't stand your simple, country mind—you haven't twigged, even yet! His name is Luc,' she spat. 'He's Philippe and Diana le Trebisonne's son. Luc le Trebisonne. Your stepbrother.' She laughed at Claire's shock, her mouth a blurred gash of scarlet in front of Claire's dazed eyes. 'Your father destroyed Trader's mother——' Claire gasped and Phoenix paused in triumph. And Claire was remembering what Trader had said: that her father had destroyed his mother.

It was true! 'Oh, the penny's dropping,' sneered Phoenix. 'Here's more: your father deprived Trader of his rightful inheritance. Ever since he was a seething, explosive fifteen-year-old, Trader's been set on taking revenge on Jack Jardine for what he did to the Trebisonne family. *Now* do you believe me?'

Claire sank back into the seat, her body suddenly heavy as lead. Trader. Luke—or, rather, it would be the French spelling, Luc, if it was an old Jersey family. And Trader had said there was one more thing he had to do.

Wreak revenge on the Jardines.

'Get out of the car,' goaded Phoenix. 'Leave, before he hurts you any more—because he will! He has such degradation in store for you that you'll never survive it! Run!' she urged. 'Here, take this . . .' Claire stared at the money, piling up in her lap. 'Grab the next plane home and lick your wounds with your mother——'

'My mother?' She jerked into life again. 'My mother's here, in Jersey——'

'No!' said Phoenix maliciously. 'Your father dumped her again——'

'Oh, poor Mother!' groaned Claire.

'Lucky, I reckon! She scuttled back home to those ghastly aunts of yours, tail between her legs. So should you. Go home!' Phoenix reached over and opened the door.

The urge to flee was instinctive, the suggestion tempting. Claire put one foot on the tarmac and then her mind began to tick over. She resisted the shove that Phoenix gave her, withdrew her leg and concentrated hard on making her whirling brain work.

'Hurry!' screamed Phoenix. 'He'll be back soon, for God's sake——'

'*Shut up!*' yelled Claire furiously. 'I've got to think——'

'There's no time——'

To her own amazement, Claire rounded on Phoenix and caught her shoulders, shaking the woman with a violence she'd never known before. 'Listen to me,' she hissed menacingly. 'Keep your mouth shut for a few moments or I swear, I'll break the habit of a lifetime, totally lose my temper and flatten you!'

In disgust, she pushed the astounded woman away and shut her out of her mind. There were more important things to deal with than slapping the malicious Phoenix. So she conjured up images of Trader into her head. How he'd looked at her. How he'd behaved, the way he'd sounded, the way he'd touched her, cherished her...

When she'd had doubts, there had been explanations before that made sense. She owed him a chance. With a straightening of her body and a renewed sense of purpose, Claire said quietly, 'He loves me and I love him. I don't know why you can't see that and why you're being so vicious towards me when I've done nothing to you——'

'So it's war?' grated Phoenix.

Claire flicked her a quick glance. 'War,' she agreed coldly.

'No woman's ever been able to take him away from me before.'

'Because you fed them with lies, I imagine,' Claire said shrewdly in answer to the terrible boast, and Phoenix shrugged. Inside, Claire felt ice-cold. The woman was dangerous, if she'd seen off all opposition until now. It occurred to Claire that Trader adored his childhood friend and was so loyal that he might not believe anything adverse about her. She couldn't appeal to him for support. She was on her own. And Trader was hurrying towards them already!

'Hi! Pass the keys, Fee.' He grinned at them both and slipped into the driver's seat. 'And now, Claire, we're driving somewhere very special. Come and sit next to me, darling.' Both she and Phoenix opened their doors, and Trader laughed in delight. 'I'll have to call you something else, Fee! Claire is "darling" now! How do you fancy "poppet"?' he asked indulgently.

'Not a lot.' However angry she might be by Trader's invitation to Claire, Phoenix still kept grinning warmly. 'I think,' she said, as Claire slid in beside Trader and stretched up to kiss his smiling mouth, 'you'll be changing your affections when you hear what I've been up to.'

He flicked on the ignition and began to drive out of the compound. 'Oh, what?'

'Wait till we get to our destination,' Phoenix answered smugly.

Claire worried. Something was in the wind. The suspense made her pulses race. Yet she chatted gaily to Trader, remarking on the gentle countryside and the gorgeous honey-coloured Jersey cattle with their huge black eyelashes, despite the tension creeping into her body. It scared her that something was yet to unfold which could threaten her marriage.

Except she wouldn't allow that! She'd fight tooth and nail for Trader. Anyone, *anyone* who stood in her way would find that even a gentle, easygoing softie could turn tigress if her man was being dragged away by some gaudy predator!

Her eyes glinted as green as the emerald grass of inland Jersey. A battle! She and Phoenix would fight it out without Trader even knowing—and she would win. Of that she was certain.

He began to tell her a little about the island's history. And she could hear the love in his voice, the wistfulness—and that tense excitement that pervaded the very pores of his body. But she didn't push him. He'd tell her the reason for his elation soon enough. Her curiosity would wait.

'Different beaches here from Palm Island, as you can see,' he said softly, waving a loving hand at the rich, golden sands ahead. Dark, jagged rocks rose in the sea beyond, rocks which became islands further out. And on the great expanse of beach, tractors were collecting seaweed. 'But just as beautiful.'

'They are,' she agreed huskily, squeezing his hand where it lay on her thigh. 'Perhaps we'll have time for a stroll, before we...change for supper?' she suggested.

Trader's breath shuddered in. She knew from the way he shifted that he had remembered the last time they'd 'changed for supper' and his loins were contracting in reaction to her deliberate seduction. 'I can't think of anything I'd rather do,' he growled.

'I can,' broke in Phoenix tartly from the back.

He shot Claire a quick, alarmingly wary look. 'In my own time, Fee,' he muttered roughly. 'In my own time.'

'Can't you tell me where we're going?' coaxed Claire.

He lifted her hand and kissed it. 'Yes, darling. I can. It's a house I've loved all my life. A house I've coveted and fought for with every fibre of my being, every breath in my body.'

Cold chills of an irrational dread crawled down Claire's spine. 'A...house?' she repeated, astonished to see that his eyes were misty with a deep emotion.

'Not an ordinary house,' he said softly. 'It's the reason I'm on edge, Claire. Can you imagine, wanting something so fiercely for twenty years that your whole life has been directed to attaining it?'

'No,' she answered apprehensively.

'It was my father's house,' he said, unaware that she knew who he was. She drew in a silent breath. He was talking about the manor house! 'It's beautiful. Warm, pink granite, a steep roof with huge chimneys, white shutters and a glorious garden. It's set a little way back from its own private beach with woods behind and a small river running through. There's an ancient dovecote which we call a colombier and which looks a bit like a huge stone drum, large enough to house four thousand doves. It has flower meadows spangled with violets and daisies, wild strawberries, periwinkles and marguerites. There's a rose garden where you reel with the scent from the old damask roses and a fountain and——'

'I think she's got the picture,' drawled Phoenix.

'Yes, I have.' Soberly, Claire thought that she knew what it looked like, anyway. It had been described to her often enough and sighed over by her mother so many times. Now she understood why Trader had been so angry that her father had taunted him by taking her mother to the manor! It also explained Trader's anger and discomfort at the wedding, hearing her father maliciously referring to 'his home, the

Trebisonne manor'. It had been a deliberate and cruel reminder on her father's part.

Yet it seemed Trader now owned the house! Fearful of what might have happened, she realised that Trader was laughing with Phoenix.

'You're brilliant,' he was saying to her.

'Grateful to me?' asked Phoenix slyly.

'Grateful? Wait till we stop!' grinned Trader. 'I'll kiss you so hard, you'll damn well fall over!'

'Trader!' gasped Claire.

'We're nearly there!' he said, ignoring her. 'Hell, I don't know if you two know what this means to me! It's——'

'Everything you've always wanted,' provided Phoenix, almost purring like a cat.

Claire felt her stomach lurch. But he wasn't listening. He'd stopped the car and was staring ahead at a huge mellow stone archway. Above the arch was carved a stone with the date: 1623. And to one side...

'Le Trebisonne,' she whispered.

'Yes!' he breathed. 'I am——'

'I know who you are,' she rasped. 'Phoenix told me.'

'Damn you, Fee!' he complained without any real rancour. He was bubbling, simmering like a cheerful volcano, ready to explode with delight.

'Does...does my father know?' she asked nervously.

'No. That had to be kept a secret till I had eased the manor from his greedy paw,' growled Trader. 'He has never linked me with the skinny little runt who always got under his feet. Besides,' he said coldly, 'he never made eye-contact with me when I was a kid. I think he was afraid what he'd see. I doubt he even knew what colour my eyes were. He spent as little time with my mother and me as possible. I think he loathed us both.'

Oblivious to her worried silence, Trader drove through the arch and drew up in front of the unbelievably beautiful house. Claire felt herself shaking. She could sense his overpowering emotions, the great love he felt for the house of his ancestors. And yet she knew that Phoenix was waiting to unleash some awful bombshell. Or perhaps Trader would do so himself.

Because the house had definitely belonged to her father on her wedding day. So what pressures had Trader brought to bear on her father? He'd promised not to seek revenge! And now that the house was his, would he need *her* any longer?

'I have my home. I have my revenge,' he said, his eyes glittering with silvery lights. 'After years of hard work, wheeling and dealing... My family's feudal seat,' he said, as if to himself. 'My family have been *seigneurs*—lords of Jersey—for nearly a thousand years. And now I've returned. I can't tell you what this means to me, Claire! I look forward to seeing your father's face!'

It was beginning to sink in. An awesome sense of destiny had driven Trader to this moment. Something bigger than she could ever hope to understand. Suddenly she jumped out, desperate for fresh air, the feeling of doom pressing in on her every second she sat in that car with Phoenix silently crowing in the back over some secret knowledge.

'Let's look around!' she cried, simulating cheerfulness.

'Sorry, you're barred,' drawled Phoenix, getting out.

Claire blinked. '*What*?'

'Fee——' began Trader, looking puzzled.

'It's her or me,' said Phoenix triumphantly. 'Now you choose between us.'

'Don't be daft——' Trader scathed, thinking she was joking.

Phoenix interrupted. 'When I told you on the phone-link to the plane that I'd persuaded Jardine to sell the manor, you jumped to a few hasty conclusions,' she said calmly. 'First, you were wrong to assume that Jardine and Claire's mother were still hanging around.'

Trader frowned. 'But I'll need to sign the transfer! Without Jardine I can't do that! Why aren't they here?' he demanded.

'Relax,' said Phoenix airily. 'No problem. Jardine was playing around with some local floozie and Brodie Jardine ran home. I told Claire. She knows.'

Phoenix lifted a determined chin when Trader held out his arms to Claire in an immediate gesture of sympathy. And the woman smiled nastily when Claire remained as still as a statue.

'I'm sorry if you're disappointed, darling,' said Trader softly. 'But I can't hide the fact that I'm glad Brodie had the strength to walk away. She's got Jardine's measure at last. I think she'll find happiness now.'

'Go on, Phoenix,' demanded Claire coldly.

'Facing defeat?' cooed Phoenix. 'Country girls shouldn't tangle with me! You see, Trader, I persuaded Jardine to sell the manor——'

'I know,' he said impatiently. 'Come to the point! What's the problem?'

'The problem is, darling, that he's already sold it. But not to you.'

Claire watched him stagger back a step, his face ashen. He loves this place more than his own life, she thought, horrified to see his shock.

'Who!' he demanded grimly. 'Who, Fee? Tell me and I'll double their price! Anything they want they can have, but I must own le Trebisonne!' His mouth whitened with strain. 'You know what I've put into my life to achieve this! You know what it *means* to me!'

'I do,' soothed Fee. Her mouth curved into a huge, self-satisfied smile. 'You needn't worry, darling. I borrowed the money myself. Trebisonne belongs to me.'

'Oh, God!' Claire whispered. She knew now. A carrot. His house was to be dangled in front of his nose as a temptation. 'That's the choice. Little Claire and Boston, or alluring Phoenix and Le Trebisonne!' she said hoarsely.

He was speechless, his eyes narrowing as they flicked from the icy Claire to the triumphant Phoenix. Then he jerked around and stared at the house with haunted eyes, panting heavily as though someone had kicked the breath from his body.

The hairs on Claire's neck lifted. To her utter dismay, he began to walk forward, stopping when he reached the huge oak door. His hand reached out and he stroked it lovingly. Phoenix threw Claire a scornful look and swayed up to Trader, unlocking the door and pushing it open invitingly.

'I love you, Trader,' said Claire in her soft, melodious voice. 'I love you now and I will love you whatever happens to you, whatever your fortunes.' His back stiffened and, when he turned, she could see the pain driving through his body.

'You and I could be happy,' husked Phoenix. 'You know I've loved you all my life——'

'Oh, Fee,' he breathed. And whether his eyes closed in ecstasy or despair, Claire had no way of knowing. But she felt more afraid than she ever had, in the whole of her life. The warm sunshine made the afternoon hum. And the silence intensified, with nothing but the gulls wheeling and screaming overhead to break the tension. Then Trader touched Phoenix gently on the arm. 'Go inside, Fee,' he said hoarsely. 'I have something to say to Claire.'

'Sure. Don't be long, *dahling*. I want us to look around our house together. You and me. Everyone else can go to hell!'

'Fee,' he growled. 'Fee . . .'

Claire mustered all her love for Trader and sent it to him in a message through her eyes. His jaw was clenched tightly and her heart ached for him. But he mustn't choose the house. He *had* to choose her!

'Trader——' she croaked, and found herself unable to get another word beyond her parched throat. So she pleaded again with her eyes.

'I can't believe what's happened,' he rasped. 'It's been my lifetime's ambition to live here. To marry and preserve my dynasty.'

'As your father did.' Philippe le Trebisonne had married a woman he didn't love for the dynasty! What would Trader do to continue the bloodline? 'But your parents were so unhappy,' she pointed out, firmly, yet gently. 'And you, their child, grew up in an emotional desert.'

'That's why I gave my love to the house,' he explained softly, caressing the carved stone pillar that supported the portico. 'And, incidentally, why I'm fond of your mother. She gave me the only love I ever had when I was small. I'd sit on her knee and she'd let me help her make pastry and we'd lick the cake bowl out together. She told me stories, she hugged me when I fell over and loved me like her own son.'

'Oh, Trader!' Claire's eyes filled with tears for the sad, lonely boy in the beautiful and heartless house. 'That was the reason for those looks you and she exchanged every now and then! I'm glad she gave you comfort. I knew something had upset her terribly when she'd worked at the house, because she couldn't speak about it.'

'I hope you can understand why I have hated your father so deeply,' he said harshly. 'When he married my mother, I knew he didn't love her. And he taunted me with that knowledge, aware that I couldn't tell my mother how he really felt.' A shuddering breath ran through his body and his mouth twisted bitterly. 'We were reading *Lady Chatterley's Lover* at school,' he growled. 'You can imagine the teasing I had to suffer.'

'Awful,' she sobbed, knowing she'd be red-nosed and ugly in a few moments, but quite unable to stop the tears.

'My mother shut herself away,' went on Trader quietly. 'I thought she'd rejected me. It wasn't true; she was just utterly miserable. At her funeral, I discovered she'd died of acute liver failure. She'd drunk herself to death.'

'Oh, the poor woman!' murmured Claire sadly.

'I imagine she'd learnt that your father was being unfaithful.' Trader leaned against the pillar as if he had no energy left in his body. 'For years after, I blamed myself for not noticing her condition. I'd been wrapped up in my own miseries and I hadn't seen her often. She'd hidden her condition well but, looking back, I recognise the signs. That's why I hold Jack Jardine responsible for my mother's death,' he said through his teeth.

Small pinpricks of alarm lifted the hairs on her skin. Revenge. It was deeply embedded in his heart. Deep enough to... She gulped. He was a proud man and had spent a lifetime preparing for this moment. He was close to achieving the ultimate prize: wresting the house from her father. And bitterness sat in his mind like a canker.

She remembered with a qualm that he'd said his vice was tenacity. He would never give up le Trebisonne. The realisation stopped her tears.

'You'd sell your soul,' she whispered, appalled, remembering what he'd said. 'Raw survival, mow down your enemies——'

'I'd never give up what I value most in the world,' he said quietly.

'Nor will I,' she snapped in determination. And walked towards him. 'You're not the only one with tenacity!' She put her arms around his neck, kissing him with all the passion of a woman who is about to have her lover torn away from her. 'I love you,' she whispered in his mouth.

'Trader!' screamed Phoenix from a window somewhere above them. 'Haven't you finished yet?'

He pushed Claire away and she closed her eyes in despair. 'Yes. We've finished. Claire——'

'*No!*' She glared. 'You can't do this! We love each other, you know we do! I won't let you walk in there!' She tossed her head at the gleam in his black eyes. 'How dare you throw away your only chance of happiness?' she declared angrily. 'I'm worth a million of that scheming, conniving, devious, self-centred Phoenix! Your right hand? She's a hook, steel to the core and grafted on to you for so long you don't even realise that you've got a dangerous weapon flailing around that could hurt you if you don't duck!'

Trader's mouth quivered. 'Claire——' he began, sounding rather stupefied.

'Don't interrupt!' she yelled. 'Come back with me to Ireland——'

'If I don't?' he murmured.

'I'll—I'll—I'll knock you on the head and drag you off!' she threatened wildly.

'How can I refuse?' he drawled, opening his hands in a gesture of defeat. 'Not that I was going to, anyway.' He smiled at her sudden, poleaxed silence, and wistfully touched the wall of the house just once more with the very tips of his fingers. 'Goodbye, le Trebisonne,' he said huskily. 'May God protect you.'

'Tr... Tr...' Nothing worked. Not her throat, her feet, her body—all seemed to be in a state of shock.

'Trader,' he said firmly, as if to a child. 'The man who loves you. Remember? The man whose life you are about to change. Who has been on a knife's edge ever since you agreed to marry him.' He took Claire in his arms, kissing away her bewildered frown. 'It's over,' he said gently. 'The doubts, the fears, the tensions. Poor Phoenix. She's lost herself the best friend she ever had. I never knew how she felt. As for my pursuit of your father, I think he'll destroy himself—

he won't need any help from me. A man who would lie to his daughter for his own ends isn't worth the effort.'

'You—you're choosing *me*?' she gasped.

Trader chuckled. 'How could I not? Ever since I first saw you, you've meant everything to me. And I've never known such happiness as I've shared with you.' His mouth brushed her hair. 'I can't tell you how upset I was when I thought that you and your father had decided to make a marriage arrangement with me to keep me quiet about the tax—and to get your hands on my money.'

'You were quite ruthless,' she said primly. 'Demanding sex as a payment——'

'I was determined to have anything I could,' he admitted ruefully. 'Anything, if it meant being near you. Shall we pinch Phoenix's car and drive to the airport?' he murmured. 'I know a way to pass away the time while we fly to Ireland. I think I'm interested in exploring the limits of my wife's assertiveness,' he said with a teasing smile.

She blushed. 'Why should I give you up without a fight?' she said with a grin. Then fixed him with her green eyes. 'I would have resorted to violent measures, you know, if you'd proved intractable!'

'I know!' He laughed. 'Equal passions, Claire,' he husked. 'Mutual love. We'll be so happy. I can advise Fairchilds' from an office in the home I want to build, by the beach. We can walk every day along the sand and let the wind tangle our hair and the rain soak us if it must.'

'Lovely,' she said softly, her eyes shining. 'Our children can build sandcastles there with us—and huge sand dams against the Atlantic——'

'Our children!' he said fondly. 'Your mother will make a wonderful grandmother!'

'And you will make a wonderful father,' she said shakily.

'Not unless I practise,' he said with a wicked grin.

His mouth claimed hers and her whole body flared into life as if he'd ignited her. Trader was losing control and so was she, their hands entwining, parting, clutching one another in a wild, helpless need. Poor Phoenix, she thought. And vowed to see that his lifelong friend was cared for, perhaps by Charles, because she knew what it was to love a man beyond all reason.

And to be loved back as fiercely. She smiled against his demanding mouth. She wasn't second-best. She was all he'd ever wanted. Nothing was stronger than love.

'Let's go home,' she said softly. 'Home to Ballymare.'

Coming Next Month

HARLEQUIN PRESENTS®

#1821 UNWANTED WEDDING Penny Jordan
(Top Author)
Rosy had to be married within three months. Guard Jamieson
was successful, sexy—and single. With no other candidate
available to walk her down the aisle, it looked as if Rosy would
have to accept Guard's offer to help her out.

#1822 DEADLY RIVALS Charlotte Lamb
(Book Two: SINS)
When Olivia first met Max she was utterly captivated. But Max
was her father's business enemy and she was forbidden to see
him again. Four years later she agreed to marry Christos, Max's
nephew. Then Max returned to claim her....

#1823 TWO'S COMPANY Carole Mortimer
(9 TO 5)
Juliet's boss has left her half his company but she has to
share it with Liam, his son, who is sure that she seduced
his father. Nor does she want him to know that she was
engaged to his despised younger brother. Will he find out
her dark secret?

#1824 A SAVAGE BETRAYAL Lynne Graham
(This Time, Forever)
Mina and Cesare had met again, four years after he rejected
her as a gold-digging tramp! Now he was determined to
marry her, but only to pursue his revenge on Mina.

#1825 SPRING BRIDE Sandra Marton
(Landon's Legacy: Book 4)
Kyra's father's legacy would allow her to assert her independence. Antonio would help her—but at a price! He wanted to
own her completely—and if she succumbed Kyra knew she
would never be free again.

#1826 PERFECT CHANCE Amanda Carpenter
(Independence Day)
Mary's life was reasonably happy—until the day
Chance Armstrong walked into it! He was offering her the
perfect chance for a lot of excitement and the most exciting
challenge of all.... He asked Mary to marry him!

BRIDE'S BAY RESORT

UNLOCK THE DOOR TO GREAT ROMANCE AT BRIDE'S BAY RESORT

Join Harlequin's new across-the-lines series, set in an exclusive hotel on an island off the coast of South Carolina.

Seven of your favorite authors will bring you exciting stories about fascinating heroes and heroines discovering love at Bride's Bay Resort.

Look for these fabulous stories coming to a store near you beginning in January 1996.

Harlequin American Romance #613 in January
Matchmaking Baby by Cathy Gillen Thacker

Harlequin Presents #1794 in February
Indiscretions by Robyn Donald

Harlequin Intrigue #362 in March
Love and Lies by Dawn Stewardson

Harlequin Romance #3404 in April
Make Believe Engagement by Day Leclaire

Harlequin Temptation #588 in May
Stranger in the Night by Roseanne Williams

Harlequin Superromance #695 in June
Married to a Stranger by Connie Bennett

Harlequin Historicals #324 in July
Dulcie's Gift by Ruth Langan

Visit Bride's Bay Resort each month wherever Harlequin books are sold.

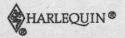

HARLEQUIN ®

BBAYG